NICK & CO. C

'I'm sure they are dumping waste straight into the canal,' Sam said. 'I think we should look at those pipes we saw.'

The gang murmured in agreement—so Sam outlined her plan.

The canal used to be a great place for fishing, but now there's no sign of life in the murky water. Nick & Co. are determined to find out who is behind the pollution. But, as usual, nothing goes quite as the gang has planned . . .

Bob Croson, the author, is married to Jean, an artist, and they have two sons, Bill and Ben.

NICK & CO
CLEAN UP

Bob Croson

A LION PAPERBACK
Oxford · Batavia · Sydney

Published by
Lion Publishing plc
Sandy Lane West, Oxford, England
ISBN 0 7459 2345 3
Albatross Books Pty Ltd
PO Box 320, Sutherland, NSW 2232, Australia
ISBN 0 7324 0746 X

First edition 1993

A catalogue record for this book is available
from the British Library

Printed and bound in Great Britain
by Cox & Wyman Ltd, Reading

Contents

1

The Beginning

I lay on my front in the warm grass, staring at the water of the canal. It was hot, and my mind drifted. I was leading my team out as Captain of England. This time we were going to win.

Suddenly a voice jolted me out of my dreams.

'Hey, Nick, you've got a bite!' It was Sparky, my best pal.

At last! My eyes quickly focused and, sure enough, the line was bobbing in the murky water. I leapt to my feet, grabbed the rod from its rest, and pulled. The rod bent as I heaved, but the fish didn't appear.

'This is a big one,' I yelled at nobody in particular.

I pulled harder. The rod bent until I thought it might break. Suddenly there was a *whoosh*, and the fish leapt from the water, and jammed in the tree behind me. Only it wasn't a fish, it was a grimy old trainer, and it neatly wrapped my line round a branch.

'Oh, fishhooks!' I grumbled.

I shot a look along the canal bank. I knew the rest of the gang were trying not to laugh. They were deliberately not looking at me. When I turned to rescue my line, I could hear stifled giggling, but every time I turned round it stopped. If there's one thing I can't stand, it's being laughed at.

After a lot of impatient tugging I sorted everything out and threw the trainer into the bushes. I lay back again in the grass and tried to get back to some serious dreaming. But my concentration had been shattered. I looked along at the gang now back at their fishing. We were the best gang in the whole city, even though I said it myself. Our youth club was brilliant, all planned by ourselves with the help of our local church.

Sparky, my best pal, sat just along from me, patiently waiting for the fish to bite. He was a good friend who never let me down. Then there was Chip. He was a computer freak, and had invented all sorts of gadgets to help him, but he still had no fish. Next to him was Raj. Even though he was the brightest and fittest guy I knew, he had no fish either. Then Whizzer. He was never going to catch anything. His fishing rod was jigging about in time to his Walkman. He spent most of his time in a world of his own, never still, always moving to the music in his earphones.

Nobody was having any success. My dad said that when he was a lad there were hundreds of fish here. I didn't believe that, it was just father-speak, his memory going funny in his old age. Mind you, I didn't want to go home empty-handed for him to gloat!

Further along the bank my sister Little Mo sat with my girlfriend Sam, who was Sparky's sister. Sam was better than most of the gang at most sports, but was bored stiff with fishing. She had also gone vegetarian, and wouldn't eat fish. She said she didn't like the thought of the fish being hurt.

The other day I told her it was because she was a silly female—a bad choice of words. She pushed me into a dustbin on the High Street and wrote 'stupid sexist' on the bin with a piece of chalk before walking off. 'Who looks silly now?' she said. It took me ages to get out with the rest of the gang laughing and not helping. Sometimes I wonder why I like her so much. Still—that's me all over. Speak first, think later.

'There's an awful smell around here,' Sam called out.

'Well, it's not me,' I shouted back.

'Oh, ha ha,' she replied.

'Canals smell like that,' Lump butted in knowingly.

Lump was the final member of the gang. His parents owned the local chip shop and he loved them both, the parents and the chips, that is! Mind you, he loved anything edible, and it showed.

Everyone returned to what they were doing. Lump had two huge plastic tubs beside him. In one was a pile of maggots for fishing. In the other was a pile of 'nibbles' which his mum had given him so that he didn't get hungry. He wasn't really interested in fishing, but it was quiet and he could eat in peace without using any energy. After all, he had all the fish he needed at home! It turned my stomach to see him tossing maggots into the canal from the tub, and then with the same hand grabbing some nibbles to shovel into his mouth. Yuck!

I had an idea.

'Sparky!' I whispered.

I nodded my head and pointed in Lump's direction, gesturing with my hands. Sparky got the idea. He put down his rod and crept along the towpath until he was behind Lump. The rest of the gang watched with growing interest. Using a stick, Sparky managed to push the two plastic boxes along just after Lump had thrown some maggots into the canal.

Lump's hand reached down for something to eat. Straight into the tub of maggots! He scooped up a handful and popped them into his mouth. There was a pause. Everyone watched in fascination. Suddenly Lump went pink, stood up, and spat the pile of maggots into the canal.

'Eugh, eugh,' he screamed, reaching for a can of Coke at his side.

We all fell about laughing.

'You pigs!' Lump shouted, between swigging mouthfuls of Coke and spitting it out.

I laughed so much I knocked my rod off its rest and it fell into the water. Eventually, when I had managed to stop laughing, my sides still aching, I looked around for my rod. It had floated away and somehow got caught in the branch of a tree overhanging the canal.

The only thing to do was to climb out along the branch to get it back. It didn't look a very healthy branch, but no one else would do it, whatever I offered. I crawled along it very, very carefully, the branch bending closer to the water with every move I made.

Before long I was lying on the branch, trying to keep my feet out of the water. Boy, it really smelled bad when you got this close. I was nearly within reach of the rod, and the branch was just inches above the water. One stretch should do it! One stretch, a slip, and . . . Whoaah! I fell with a great splash into the canal.

Lump laughed loudest!

The water was vile, and it tasted awful. Surfacing, I spat out the revolting liquid. The bottom, on which I was standing, was slimy and horrible. I reached in among the branches and retrieved the rod. Suddenly I saw a dead fish floating there. Thinking quickly, I pulled out the fish and claimed it.

'First catch of the day,' I yelled triumphantly. I dragged myself out of the water with the gang's help, holding the fish and rod.

'Whew, what a stink!' Sam said. 'You can throw that poor fish back. You never caught it. Looks like it's been dead for ages.'

I looked at it. Out of the water it did look grim. Its scales were flaking off in my hand. No way was I going to get away with this. I threw it back. It was time to go.

'See you later at the club,' I called out as we went our separate ways.

Sparky, Sam and Mo helped me home. Sparky and Sam lived next door to Mo and me. I squelched through the streets, dreading what Mum would say! Leaving Sam and Sparky, I sneaked in the back door while Mo distracted Mum. Unfortunately, I forgot about Wally the family dog. As he jumped up to greet me, my wet shoes slipped on the kitchen floor and I made a terrible clatter as I knocked over a chair.

'Stupid Wally,' I grumbled and the poor dog slunk off to his basket. As quick as I could, I made a dive for the hall and stairs, but Mum, alerted by the noise, followed the trail of canal water.

'Nick, stop there!' she yelled.

I stood, frozen in time, on the stairs. It was the usual. First she was cross at the mess, then she was worried in case I had hurt myself, then she was cross again at the state of my clothes. Mothers!

I had a shower, got dressed and very quietly and politely excused myself to go to the youth club. I didn't feel like eating. Mum wasn't keen to let me go, but I used the tactic of backing out the door while asking, just at the moment when she was very busy getting tea for Dad coming home from work. When I got to the club everyone was already there, because I had waited for that right moment to escape.

'Hi, Nick! Heard you had a smashing—or was it splashing?—time at the canal,' Doug called across to me as I entered the club hut. Doug was the local curate and in charge of the youth club. He'd got me out of scrapes in the past. He was a good friend. But tonight I didn't feel like laughing and I just looked at him, because I couldn't think of anything to say. I wandered over to play pool with Raj. It was already late and before we had really got going Doug was calling us all over for a meeting.

'Hang on, Doug, we've only just started,' I complained.

'I can't help it if you decided to go for a late afternoon dip in the canal,' Doug replied. 'We've got a lot to discuss.'

Grumpily I joined the others.

'I've got some stuff here from the City Council,' Doug started. 'It's about this year's City Festival, and there are lots of things for youth clubs to get involved in.'

'Waste of time,' I grumbled. I was feeling a bit off, and also fed up at missing out on my game of pool.

Doug ignored me and went on to describe the events. 'Poetry competition. Painting competition. Fancy dress,' he started. I couldn't believe my ears. Nick and Co. doing things like that! Over my dead body. 'A float in the parade. Raft race. Music competition,' he went on.

'Hang on, hang on,' I butted in. My head was hurting and I was cross. 'We're not doing things like that.'

'Why not?' Doug asked.

'Because,' I began.

'No, you hang on,' Sam interrupted crossly. 'Some of the things sound fun.' The others nodded in agreement and looked excited.

I folded my arms and scowled but they all ignored me. There was a lot of discussion and eventually they agreed they would build a float for the parade, and make a raft to enter the raft race. They also wanted to enter the music competition, as long as it could be a 'rap'—that was Whizzer's favourite and he started getting enthusiastic. He danced about, clicking his fingers. Lump joined in and it really looked funny.

In spite of how I felt I started to laugh. I laughed so much I began to feel sick. Doug looked across to me. 'Are you all right, Nick?' he asked. 'You look a bit green.'

I felt it. Ever since leaving home to come to the club I had been feeling more and more sick. I hadn't eaten anything but that feeling of being full to the brim and ready to burst was suddenly unavoidable. The last bit of laughter had finished me off. I just looked at Doug, and made a furious dash for the nearest door, keeping my mouth shut. The first door was the store cupboard. When you're feeling like throwing up you seem to lose your senses. I lurched to the next door, the toilet, and just made it.

Sam helped me clean up, and then Doug and Sam took me home in Doug's van. I was feeling better, but still had a bit of a headache. I felt quite weak. There was me expecting lots of sympathy, and my mum just forced medicine down my throat.

'Yeukk!' I protested. But I was packed off to bed. Sam and Doug came up to see me.

'I think he'll be all right now,' Mum said to them. 'If he's not I'll call the doctor, although I think he would condemn this room as a health hazard if he came.' She looked around in disgust. Doug and Sam looked round and agreed with Mum. It was a bit of a mess, I admit.

'This room's an environmental disaster,' Sam said.

I looked at her, at Doug, then at Mum, and threw up in the waste-paper bin!

2
Speedy Disaster

The doctor said it must have been something I ate. My mum said I must have done something stupid, again. My dad said I probably caught it from something in my room. Well, I hadn't eaten anything different from the stuff I normally eat. I never do anything stupid! And as for my room, the dirt and dust was just there to protect my belongings. Some of my collections would be worth a lot one day. It must have been something else.

After the next morning in bed I was allowed out again, and felt perfectly all right. The next day at the club I had a good game of table tennis against Sparky, which I won. That made me feel right back on top form. We sat down for a can of drink, and Sam came across.

'I think you got sick from drinking canal water,' she said. 'I don't think I've ever seen anything quite so disgusting.'

'Oh, I don't know,' Sparky chipped in. 'Haven't you seen Nick's collection of unwashed socks? They must have walked across to greet you when you went to see him with Doug.'

I threw the table tennis ball at him. 'You may be right,' I said to Sam. 'You remember that dead fish I found?'

I was cut short by Doug calling us round to talk to us.

'Remember the City Festival we were talking about yesterday?' he said. 'Well, time's passing by and the raft race is getting nearer.' I sighed. Why was Doug stating the obvious? It was something adults were always doing.

'We've got three or four weeks,' he said. 'So we'd better start getting the building of it organized. City Festival week starts a week after the end of term.'

'*We'd* better start?' I interrupted. 'Doug, I've seen your attempts at building things!'

'And we've seen your attempts at organizing things, Nick!' Sam butted in.

I was seriously dischuffed. What an insult! Before I could think of a suitable response, Sam took over. She and Raj were going to design it. They set about it straight away. I went off to play pool with Sparky. When they got stuck, let them come back to me to sort it out. Much to my dismay, within an hour they had come up with a pretty good design. Now we had to get the materials together. We needed car inner tubes, plastic containers for floats, wood and some rope to lash it all together.

After some discussion, we agreed on who would be responsible for getting the stuff. Lump knew he could get plastic containers from his shop, and Sparky and

Raj were going round to the local tyre depots and garages to ask for inner tubes. Whizzer knew that there was some rope in the shed at the bottom of his garden. And Doug knew somebody who might help with some wood. Sam and I were given directions to a workshop in some old buildings near the canal. I laughed when Doug told me the name to look for— Leatherbarrow! Freaky!

The next Saturday, Sam and I found the workshop down Canal Street. There were a number of workshop units with their backs to the street, and their fronts onto an old canal wharf. I saw an old brick building with a sign outside: LEATHERBARROW FINE FURNITURE.

I knocked on the door but got no answer. There was the sound of very loud machinery—a lathe or something. I pushed the door open and called.

'Mr Leatherbarrow,' I said in my polite voice.

No answer. Sam tried and got the same. I was fed up with this. I drew in my breath and yelled at screaming pitch, 'MR LEATHERBARROW!'

Just as I started, the machinery stopped. Everybody called Leatherbarrow on our side of the city must have sat up with a start.

'Yes?' a quiet voice replied. I felt such an idiot. The door was pulled back and there stood a youngish woman in an old smock. She was wearing clogs, a spotted neckerchief, and had her hair tied back. What a hippie!

Sam took over. She explained who we were, and about how Doug had suggested we call, and so we were invited in. Now the machine had stopped, classical music was playing in the background, and there was a fantastic smell of wood. All around were pieces of furniture in different stages of completion. They looked a bit old-fashioned to me but were obviously well made.

'Hi! I'm Angelica,' said the woman, smiling. 'What can I do for you?,' she asked.

Sam explained about the raft race and our club and what we needed.

'I don't have much spare,' Angelica replied. 'You see, I don't want to waste the earth's resources. I'm very careful which wood I use, and I like to recycle wood from old furniture. But I'm sure I can find something to help.'

Sam was taking it all in. She was really into the environment and all that. What a pain. I could see her really getting involved. I mean, we'd done quite a lot of discussion in the club about the world, and how God made it, and how we had to look after it, but I thought Sam took it all too seriously.

'What a fantastic workshop,' she said, looking round admiringly. I just looked at the floor.

'Yes, it is quite nice,' nodded Angelica. 'There are quite a few of us working down here—pottery, crafts, that kind of thing. We nearly lost our workshops when they built that new factory up the canal. They're still trying to get us out.'

'Oh, I wish they would,' I thought to myself, sighing. As Sam and Angelica Leatherbarrow went on and on about the environment, she managed to find enough old packing-case wood to build the raft. We got it back to the club on a trolley that Angelica lent us.

'Bye,' said Angelica. 'I shall look forward to seeing your raft.'

'Bye,' said Sam.

I sort of grunted goodbye. Women!

We gathered everything together in the shed at the back of the club hut and the next few Saturdays were full of hard work. When we had finished, Doug was very impressed. We couldn't wait to launch it.

'Only one thing, though,' he said, admiring our completed work. 'How are you going to get it to the canal?'

Ah! We hadn't thought of that. Or *they* hadn't.

'Well, if you'd have let me stay in charge, this wouldn't have happened,' I said to no one in particular. The spare plastic container thrown by Sam only just missed my left ear.

At last the summer holidays came. With just a week to go, and lots of time to practise, the day of the launch arrived. We had to dismantle parts of the raft and carry it in three pieces to the canal, where we put it back together. Doug insisted on coming along. He was going to be 'safety man' on the path. He also brought Angelica along to be doubly sure. We were going to launch the raft just near Angelica's yard.

We had decided to do it properly, with a ceremony. Champagne was out of the question, and it wasn't a good idea to break a glass bottle, so we christened the raft with a can of Coke, and named it *Speedy*, a nice short name. Doug thought a better name would be *Titanic*, but we ignored him.

We had borrowed some life-jackets from school. I thought this was going over the top, but Doug insisted. We each carried an oar made from a piece of packing-case. Getting on the raft was a bit tricky. Mo got on first, in the middle at the back, where she was going to steer with the rudder. Sam and I got on at opposite sides at the front; Raj and Whizzer, the same at the back. That left Lump and Chip to sit in the middle at each side. Chip got on very gingerly and crawled over to the far side. By now we were much lower in the water, and the raft was tipping slightly with the weight of Chip on one side.

'Hurry up, Lump,' I yelled at him.

Lump was dithering on the bank, as the raft bobbed unevenly on the water.

'Ooo-err,' was his nervous reply.

'Come on,' I shouted, 'Quickly!'

I shouldn't have said quickly. Whenever Lump does anything quickly it is a disaster. He hopped from foot to foot, then made an enormous leap on to the raft. Chip, who was still settling into his seat, wobbled about and gently slid into the canal.

Lump, with a scream of, 'Help, help, I'm drowning,' slid off the other side of the raft, and stood on the bottom of the canal, in the waist-deep water. Unfortunately, Lump's great leap had broken the raft, and it split into the three sections we had rebuilt. So we all slid into the water. Instead of diving to the rescue,

Doug and Angelica just fell about laughing. Although the canal was only waist-deep and we all had life-jackets on, I would have appreciated more concern.

We dragged ourselves out of the canal, together with the bits of raft. Fortunately, none of us had swallowed the canal water this time—a near-miracle! Angelica said we could use her yard to rebuild the raft, but first we all trooped home to change, and I got another mega-wigging from my mum.

By the time we got back to the canal, Doug and Angelica had rebuilt the raft, and it looked a lot stronger. Sam was a bit upset that they had altered her design, but it was a lot better. I couldn't help noticing that Doug and Angelica seemed to be getting along very well.

It was time to get back on HMS *Speedy*. This time we put Lump on first. It worked well, and very soon we were splashing up and down the canal practising speed-rowing, with Mo shouting 'IN-OUT-IN-OUT' enthusiastically. We left the raft in Angelica's yard and made our way back to the club. Doug had to call in at church and said he would catch us up later.

There was a real lazy feeling at the club hut. As we drank squash, everyone was quiet. I was daydreaming about winning the raft race single-handed. It was taking place in the city centre—lots of bridges to negotiate.

'I am worried about the canal,' said Sam. 'Angelica thinks that there's something wrong with the water since that new factory was built.'

I came back to real life with a bump. 'That hippie

freak would see pollution in anything,' I muttered, jealous of the attention Sam was giving to her.

'Well, she'd better start in your room then,' Sam responded sharply. 'There's enough pollution in there to keep her busy for months.'

'Thanks. I'm going for a hamburger, anybody coming?' I responded huffily. If there's one thing I can't stand, it's people criticizing my room. *I* like it. And it's got nothing to do with anybody else.

Nobody offered to come with me—except Lump, of course! As we left Sam was still going on about about the environment. Good grief, I hoped she wasn't trying to make them all hippies! Half an hour later, after getting our snack, Lump and I munched our way back to the club. As we turned into Church Street we could hear music coming from the club hut, very loud. I mean, LOUD. Then I remembered. Whizzer had invited two of his brothers along to help us with our rap for the music festival. The noise was tremendous.

Just as we got to the hut, Doug came out of the church, looking very upset. He was all dressed up in his vicar's gear. He called us over.

'Quick!' he yelled. 'Get them to stop. IMMEDI-ATELY.'

He looked really flustered. Then I noticed for the first time the funeral cars parked outside the church. We ran into the hut. Inside there was a real 'jamming' session going on, with everybody dancing to the rap music. I shouted and shouted but nobody heard. I mouthed at Sam but she just laughed.

The only thing I could do was run over to the

power points and pull the plugs out. It was like bursting a balloon. Everything tumbled to a stop. I was not popular! Whizzer's brothers cornered me.

'Hey man, why d'you do that?' they growled.

I gulped and pointed out of the window at the parked cars.

'It all sounded fantastic,' I crawled. 'But I don't think it fitted the words of the hymns!'

3
The Raft Race

The raft race was at the start of the City Festival week. We had spent the week before putting the finishing touches to our raft. Angelica had been very good and let us keep it in her yard. She was an odd sort of person, but generous. What I didn't like was the fact that Sam worshipped the ground she walked on, just because she kept spouting on about the environment. If I heard much more about saving the earth, I would bury myself in it!

We had painted our raft and put some flags on it. It looked really cool. The race this year started from the opposite end of the city and finished at the bridge in the city centre. Rather than row it all the way to the start, Doug and Angelica helped put it in Angelica's truck and drove us all there.

Getting the raft into the water was hard work, but we were soon milling around among a whole group of rafts. As usual, the 'adults' were all in fancy dress. I do not understand why grown men think it funny to dress up as fat ladies, and women as naughty schoolgirls.

Sam thought it was disgusting and sexist. I just thought it was yukky!

We were there to win, not to make idiots of ourselves. While the grown-ups were thrashing around, splashing each other and shouting and giggling very loudly, we manoeuvred ourselves to the front. I got quite a shock when I passed one raft.

'Hello, Nick,' a voice called out.

It came from a raft filled with grown-ups dressed as silly policemen. What next? Then I did a double-take. They *were* policemen and the one that had called out my name was Dad's boss, Inspector Sims. Good grief! He was normally such a 'normal' sort of person. Now he was acting like a complete idiot, jumping up and down on a very unstable raft made out of oil cans. I shall never understand grown-ups!

At the front there were three other rafts, all taking things seriously, and not a grown-up among them! We were all rivals, and honour was at stake. There was a lot of pushing and shoving to get the best place on the start line, and quite a bit of shouting.

'What do you call that?' Anne Calder yelled across. She was the very aggressive leader of City Youth Club. We knew her from school.

'*Speedy*,' Sam called back. And then, quick as a flash, 'What's yours called, *Sinker*?'

I was keeping out of this. I looked across in admiration at Sam, who was pushing their raft out of the way with her foot. I wasn't sure this was the wisest way to treat them as they were bigger than us, but I wasn't going to argue. Sam was raring to go.

The Mayor fired a starting pistol, and we were off. Three adults fell off their rafts pretending to be shot. Well, I suppose *they* thought it was funny. The canal was fairly straight into town, but narrowed to go under a couple of bridges. Unfortunately, one of those bridges came very quickly after the start.

There was a terrific thrashing of water as we all fought to get to the bridge first. We were in the middle, with City Youth Club on one side, and Wade Road Methodist Club on the other. Behind us, and fighting to get through, were the Scouts. You could hardly see for spray, and the shouting was tremendous.

'Come on, come on, we're winning!' was the shout from all of the front three rafts.

The Scouts were bumping along behind, banging into the back of us and the Methodists. Suddenly there was a yelp. With all the pushing and shoving, one of the metal drums that made up the Methodists' raft came adrift. Their ropes slackened and the whole raft just disintegrated, throwing them all into the water. We didn't need to stop to rescue them. There were people all along the canal from the local canoe clubs to do that. So now, there were just three at the front, all paddling furiously for the first bridge, and only two would get through.

The Scouts had obviously built their raft very well. It even had plastic seats on it. They were all working together and were gradually drawing past us. One guy was being very enthusiastic and standing up to shout and keep everyone together. We were just all paddling as hard as we could, except for Lump, who was complaining all the time.

Just at that point on the canal, there were a number of overhanging trees. The Scouts, or at least one of them, forgot this. Scouts are usually very enthusiastic about everything. This team was no exception. They were paddling extremely hard with their heads down, except for this guy facing backwards, standing up and shouting in time. Spray was everywhere. For some reason he turned, but he was too late to miss his personal disaster.

'Come on, come on, come ... Whooaah!' he yelled as he hit an overhanging branch and stuck there like an overweight magpie. Their raft, now out of balance and without a leader, crashed into the bank, yards from the bridge, allowing the two teams left to scrape through.

Just!

The City Youth Club were being a bit unfriendly, chopping at our boat and paddles with theirs, and shouting abuse at us. We had always had friendly rivalry, but they just didn't like all the publicity we got, and were now determined to beat us, whatever it took!

After the bridge, Mo sensibly steered away from them, so that we could have a clear run. However, they steered over to our side and tried to edge us into the bank. The spectators were yelling and shouting, so they couldn't do it too much, but it was obvious what they intended. Unfortunately just then we came to a short stretch where there were no spectators. As we passed between the woodyard and the new County

Court, I knew there would be trouble.

Anne Calder was determined in particular to get Sam, and Sam was determined to beat her. We were neck and neck. They brought their raft over towards us again.

'Come on. Harder, harder,' I screamed at the gang, but we couldn't get ahead. City closed on us and banged against the side of our raft. Our legs were safe on the raft, but it was still a shock for Whizzer, Lump and Sam, and Lump nearly lost his paddle.

'Whoa, hey, get off,' he shouted.

One of the kids on their raft swatted at him with an oar, but missed. I had never seen Lump move so fast. They had stopped rowing to smash into us. Whizzer and Sam pushed them away, and we took the chance to get ahead. Now we were in front and they were even more cross. I didn't think we would get away with that tactic again and was ready for trouble.

It came.

One of the City Club lads was a county swimmer. He jumped off their raft, swam up to us and grabbed the back of our raft, pushing Mo out of the way. Before we knew what was happening he was rocking us about.

We had never really got our raft to be as stable as it should be, and this rocking brought disaster. Whizzer and Raj stopped paddling and turned to deal with the intruder. Mo had fallen into the middle, arms and legs flying everywhere. The kerfuffle at the back made us even more unstable and continued to throw Mo about. One of her feet hit Chip on the shoulder and knocked him flying into the water. Then her arms flailed into Lump, who took action to get out of the way. He didn't want to end up in the canal again so he leapt forward. Unfortunately, that was where Sam was sitting.

Lump always reacts without thinking! When he hit Sam that made us even more unstable and both Sam and Lump cartwheeled into the water. The rest of us clung to the wreckage as the other raft passed us, picking up their 'pirate' on the way.

I was a bit worried because we lost Sam for a bit, and I was relieved to see her swimming back. Very quickly, some of the safety people were on the scene. They weren't interested in our anger at the cheating—they thought it was a laugh. Typical adults! But they did help us get sorted out and on our way again. I was angry, but Sam had a smile on her face.

'What are you laughing at?' I demanded. 'I don't like not winning.'

'Wait and see,' she replied, 'But let's get going. We've got to beat the Scouts. They're coming up behind us.'

I looked, and sure enough, they were heading our way. We got going, watching the City Club in the distance, heading for the victory line. There was one more bridge, and then the finish. No way would we catch them!

Then I noticed an oil barrel floating past, then another. I looked up from my paddling to see City's raft falling apart and bodies slipping into the water. I looked across at Sam, who was roaring with laughter.

'What have you done?' I demanded.

'Well, you know our first attempt fell apart because we relied on one rope holding everything together?' she replied, 'I think they made the same mistake. I just helped to show them what they had done wrong!'

When she had been thrown in the water, Sam had taken the chance to pull loose the rope that held City's raft together! My admiration for Sam grew. If there's one thing I've learned from Sam, it's that it's rubbish to say, *boys are better*. She just keeps proving it isn't true. Everyone is good at something. Even Lump must be good at *something*!

The rescue people insisted on pulling the City kids out of the water, so they couldn't do anything except shake their fists! We paddled on to triumph, and the cheers of the crowd at the finish line.

Doug and Angelica cheered us in, and gave us towels and dry clothes. I let Sam collect the prize from the Mayor, and she held the trophy up for the local newspaper to take pictures. She waved at Anne Calder, who burst into tears of anger! We gave the twenty-pound prize to Doug for club funds and headed home to dry off.

The next day at church we were asked to show the rest of the congregation our trophy. We all got a clap for our efforts. The churchwarden then stood up with 'an important announcement'. The factory by the canal was giving a large sum of money to the rebuilding programme for our church hall.

I usually let this sort of thing just wash over me. But

Sam took the announcement seriously.

'Even trying to buy the local church,' she grumbled in my ear. I had a real job holding her down. She wanted to stand up and complain. I thought it was a lot of fuss about nothing. The church needed a new hall, and here was someone willing to cough up the money to help.

Before Sam had the chance to get really huffy, Doug got up to speak. 'I want to talk today about "Caring for the world we live in".'

I could feel Sam bristling next to me. I knew it wasn't because she disagreed with Christians looking after the world. It was because of the factory. I listened as Doug talked about God creating the world and making people in his own image. But people chose to go against God and do bad things instead of good. One of the results was the badness inside people, and another was the earth suffering from that badness.

It's true, when you look around, there's so much badness caused by what people *do*. The trouble is, a lot of what seems bad, like pollution caused by cars, is part of the way we live, and it's very hard to change. 'We can't hope to change the world we live in without changing the "pollution" inside people's hearts,' he said, finishing with, 'The only way of doing that is by letting God deal with it.'

I had to admit it, he was right. We have made a real mess of God's world. Trouble is, most of us are too lazy or selfish to do anything. And the others—well, they do go on a bit. As for 'pollution in our hearts', I knew I hadn't a word to say for myself. I was sorry I was so horrible to people sometimes, and so big-headed.

On the way out, Sam was still chuntering on about the factory and accepting their 'polluted' money. She turned to me. 'Doug doesn't really understand it yet,' she said. 'But if he spends much more time with Angelica he soon will.'

It suddenly clicked. That's why Doug had seemed so distant recently, and why he had a sudden interest in the environment—because of Angelica.

I tried to be nice to Sam. She was in a bad mood. I even offered to buy her a Coke, but she wasn't interested. I walked home with her, trying to sound keen on all this environment stuff.

'Oh push off,' she snapped. 'Don't talk to me about pollution until you've sorted out that environmental disaster you call your room.'

She gave me a push and I fell through our front hedge. Right on to the patch of nettles that Dad had told me to dig up last week!

4
The Dustbin Rap

The only thing I ever did successfully in music at school was get sent out of class. Mrs Davis, our music teacher, looked on me as a disaster area in her lesson, and was convinced that I sang out of tune deliberately. I didn't. I am one of the few people asked not to sing at a football match because I put the crowd off!

So when the gang decided to enter the music competition, I had been less than enthusiastic. Inside, I was worried about what it might do to the gang's street cred. I could just imagine what City Youth might say. But most of the others were keen, and when a 'rap' was suggested, I had allowed myself to be persuaded. I said that I would join in on the day, but only in the background. And for everybody's sake, I was going to mime.

Sam had deliberately asked me not to come along to a lot of the practices because she thought my attitude would put the others off. That was fine by me, I much preferred to kick a ball about rather than practise singing. Whizzer's brothers had helped set up the backing tape and organized the music, but most of the ideas came from Sam. The theme for the music contest was to do with 'a better city', and Sam had written a rap about pollution, the environment, and all that sort of stuff.

The night before the contest I hadn't even learned the words. 'You really are a selfish slob,' complained Sam. 'Everybody else has spent hours practising to get it right, and you've hardly done anything. If you wreck it, I'll never speak to you again.'

I got the message. I went away and learnt my little bit. One thing I wasn't going to do was cross Sam. That night I decided I was definitely going to turn up on time the next morning, to set off for the competition with the rest of the gang. I couldn't work out why Mo was laughing so much at breakfast. I think she was trying to tell me something, but you never listen to younger sisters anyway. I had put on my best gear. Sunday best clothes. All very smart. I wasn't going to have Sam getting on at me. It took me a long time to get ready, and Mo went on ahead.

So, in my best gear I made my way to the club. From some distance away I could hear the noise. I opened the door and it hit me full on. Then it stopped. Everybody turned in my direction. I looked at them. They looked at me. I was in my best clothes. They were in their scruffy jeans.

There was a long silence. Then Mo started laughing and everyone joined in. I wasn't sure whether to run out, hit someone, or disappear through a crack in the floorboards. Mo came up to me and handed me an old pair of jeans—my old jeans.

'I thought you might need these,' she said.

'Why didn't you tell me?' I hissed. She just laughed.
Sisters!

Sam and Whizzer had worked out what we were
going to do. They had told me all the details. It
sounded fun, but I thought it might upset some
people—the posh sort of people who go to con-
certs. At the same time I thought I might enjoy
myself after all!

I don't think Angelica had told Doug about it either.
He looked very surprised and rather worried when we
loaded up his van with our kit, which consisted of a
dustbin and a whole heap of rubbish. I think he was a
bit upset that we all had jeans on. He obviously
expected us to turn up dressed like the church choir.
Angelica took some of us in her truck, following on
behind Doug. Whizzer held tight to his stereo system,
which was to play the backing tape.

We arrived at the Guildhall, and made our way
inside. I could see the organizers weren't keen on the
dustbin, and it took some persuading to let us bring it
in. Other 'choirs' were sitting around, all dressed up
and smart. We really looked out of place! The hall was
already filling up with people. I couldn't imagine
people volunteering to see this sort of stuff.

We had been drawn last to perform, and that meant
a huge wait, listening to everybody else, getting bored
and more nervous all the time! I felt the butterflies in
my stomach.

'Welcome to the music contest,' announced the

Mayor, who then went on for hours making a pompous speech that said nothing. Why do grown-ups do that? And why do people listen and clap? I sometimes hear people complaining about the Mayor driving around in his flash car wasting their money. Yet here they were, laughing at his terrible jokes, encouraging him to rabbit on even longer!

The contest was just as boring as I thought it would be. Our gang was completely out of place. Whizzer spent the time listening to his personal stereo, while Chip flicked through a computer magazine. Lump had brought a bag of crisps but Sam removed them from him just as he was about to open the packet.

Sparky and I had been whispering to each other and during a break in the performances a rather stuffy man with a bow tie came up. 'If you can't keep quiet,' he hissed through clenched teeth, 'you had better leave.'

I would have been quite happy to go, but Sam's look persuaded me otherwise. But we might as well have gone. I noticed a badge on the stuffy man's lapel. It read CHIEF JUDGE! Whoops!

It seemed forever before we were called to perform, but eventually we heard our name. Sam went up with the dustbin, and carefully spread junk and litter all over the stage. The audience stirred. What on earth was going on? Raj followed and put the stereo sound system down. The rest of us followed and stood or sat about among all the rubbish. I could hear the audience muttering to each other. One particular loud-voiced old lady on the front row said, 'What on earth is going on? What are those *ruffians* doing?'

Whizzer pressed the button on the tape and made everyone jump. It was enough to give someone a heart-attack. Very loudly the pre-recorded rap music started and we all moved to pick up our instruments from the carefully placed junk. First Lump turned over the dustbin and picked up a large beater made of a stick with an old bicycle inner tube wrapped round the end. Then Chip found a selection of old pans which he placed around him and played with a wooden spoon.

I picked up an old coffee tin filled with rice and started shaking it. Raj pulled out a set of bottles filled with water and played them with a metal rod. Sparky pulled two pieces of wood out of his pocket and tapped them against each other.

Mo sat at one side of the stage, and Whizzer went to the other. Sam plugged a microphone into the sound system. By now the music from our system and the home-made instruments was very loud. At a signal from Sam the music was turned down, and we quietened our playing. I daren't look at the audience. They were probably in shock!

We started the rap with a verse that we kept repeating, getting slightly louder each time:

To clean up the world, you first clean up the cidy (city);
Clean it all up and make it look priddy (pretty).

You have to rap with real rhythm and style, and Whizzer and Sam had worked hard to get us together.

Sam took hold of the mike. The rap was about the filth and dirt we all made. She had written a lot of the words herself and she really put a lot into it. And it wasn't all about bad things that people do. It was about the good things they do to help the world.

Whizzer and Mo stood up and began to dance. I knew that Whizzer was a fantastic rap dancer, but Mo was really amazing. Funny how you never realize how clever your own sister is!

When Sam had finished, she pulled out the mike and sat down. Whizzer and Mo danced off. Lump turned over his dustbin, and we all put our instruments in it and walked off. Then Raj and Sam picked up the rest of the junk and walked off with the dustbin. Whizzer came on, stopped the music, and walked off with the sound system.

The stage was empty. There was a long silence. We looked at each other. I daren't look out into the audience, where first-aiders were probably giving the kiss of life to a number of old people.

Suddenly the old lady who had complained on the front row started to clap, and very quickly everyone joined in. The applause was tremendous. We felt great—and relieved! It hadn't been easy doing an 'alternative' performance among neatly-dressed, traditional choirs.

Then came the results and the ceremony. I couldn't believe it—we were the winners! None of us had thought about what would happen next. We all went up on stage for more applause, and on the way up, we agreed that Sam and Whizzer should receive the prize.

'Thank you, everybody, for coming to this, I think you will agree, exciting and unusual music competition,' the chief judge announced, putting on a posh voice. 'The standard of music was very high, and the *panel* decided on the winners.' So he was letting us know that *he* hadn't voted for us.

'The prize,' he went on, 'has been generously donated by the Rawson Marsden Company, the latest new industry to come into our city.'

Sam wasn't so keen when she heard who was giving the prize. It was Mr Brown, the new boss at the factory by the canal. It was him who had turned up at our church and given the money to the hall building work.

We all stood there like lemons. Sam was looking like an ultra-polite lemon. Mr Brown began.

'Thank you very much for the opportunity to present a very worthwhile prize,' he said. 'We at Rawson Marsden are committed to caring for the environment.'

'Committed to talking about the environment, getting cheap publicity and polluting the environment, all at the same time,' muttered Sam under her breath. I could see her bristling. But we weren't going to miss our moment of glory. The prize was a cheque for twenty-five pounds, and a visit to the new factory.

Afterwards Sam grumbled about free publicity for 'that grotty factory', but I thought it sounded great fun. After all, it's not every day you go round a factory.

When we got back to the club, we were quickly brought back to reality. In our rush to get ready for the competition, we had created a terrible mess in the club room, and just left it. When Doug saw it he went bananas at us. It's true, we were great at talking and singing about pollution, and great at causing it! Not so great at clearing it up. I thought he was well over the top and decided to have a rest after all the hard work. Well, I shouldn't have done that.

I'd never seen Doug angry before. He didn't shout, he didn't jump up and down. But before I knew what was happening I found myself wedged in the dustbin we'd used in the competition, and no one would help me out!

5

An Environmental Disaster

The final event of the City Festival was to be a grand parade of floats through the city. After our successes in the raft race and the music contest, I wanted to make it three wins in a row. The total triumph of Nick and Co! I knew that, with a lot of work, we could win the prize for best float. It was time for me to 'take charge'.

'Right, you lot,' I called to everybody in the club hut. 'Let's get together and get this float thing sorted out.' Sam muttered something about better late than never, but I chose to ignore it. It took some time to get everybody together. But I knew just what I wanted to do.

'Sam, you check that it's OK to use Angelica's friend's lorry,' I directed. 'It won't be a problem. She's already said we can use it. Anyway, she and Doug are so gooey-eyed at the moment, she'll do anything to help us.' So Sam went off to see Angelica.

I had decided on the design for the float and started to tell the others. The theme given by the organizers was to show what each competitor had done to

41

improve the environment. In the last year we had done a sponsored litter collection and cleared an old footpath. I didn't enjoy it, but it provided a useful theme for our float now.

My idea was to build a footpath, covered with litter, going up a slope. We would then have different sorts of waste bins, and keep loading those up. We could play a tape of our winning 'rap' in the music competition, and cover the lorry with signs and banners. Finally, some of the gang could collect litter along the way. I thought the idea was great. With Sam out of the way, checking the lorry and talking to her friend Angelica, I could get on without interruption.

Raj thought the idea looked a bit risky, but before he could get going with any 'what if' and 'but' statements, I sent everybody out to gather things for the task.

When Sam found out that I had started getting things organized without her around, she was furious. But it was *my* gang. I was in charge. I liked her a lot but I wasn't having anyone take over from me.

'Stupid men,' she muttered. But she stayed with the idea. She said it was to make sure we didn't make fools of ourselves.

Later that week Sam and I called in at a café in town. We had decided to take a rest from visiting shops to beg for materials for the float.

Unfortunately, the City Club were doing the same thing. It took a lot of work to stop Sam from coming to blows with Anne Calder, who was still smarting from the disaster of their raft sinking.

'Just you watch yourselves and your crummy float,' was Anne's parting shot. From the look in her eyes she really meant it. I think she just recognized my greater intellect! With Angelica's agreement we took all of the stuff for the float to her yard. That would be safe.

It wasn't long before Sam and Angelica started making helpful suggestions. 'To help make it work,' they argued. But I had watched my mum completely change my dad's ideas without him realizing it, so I kept a careful eye on their tactics.

The Thursday and Friday before the parade was the time given to building. Everybody worked very hard with me telling them what to do, and Sam and Angelica trying to change it. But I was sticking to my plan. After all, it was *my* idea.

To make the grassy slope we used wooden boxes covered with old plywood as a base. Sam suggested that we find some of that stuff greengrocers use that looks like grass, but I wanted the real thing.

'Don't you think it will be a bit heavy and slippy?' Raj asked.

'Rubbish,' I responded. 'It's got to look real. Anyway, that lorry can take it.'

We dug up some grass and soil from the bottom of Whizzer's garden. It was a bit messy, but when it had been put on the slope it looked really good. Then I started getting carried away, demanding bushes and fences. We got the bushes from Chip's grandad—he didn't mind. But I was a bit suspicious of the fence that Whizzer brought, and he was a bit mysterious about where he got it from. Sam and Angelica made some comments about destroying the environment rather than protecting it, but the final effect was very artistic.

Trouble was, when I got down from the lorry, the only thing I could see was the bushes. It wasn't a problem for long!

Chip and Lump had been working at the top of the sloping path. Lump stood up from his work to admire the view. Then Chip got up, rather suddenly. Unfortunately, the path was only wide enough for two average-sized people. Lump was not average. When Chip got up, he knocked Lump, and Lump ... Lump ...

Put it like this. The last time I went to the seaside, I had a go on a pinball machine. Lump, travelling down the lorry, reminded me of that, but the sound effects were different. Instead of the tuneful pinging of the machine, there were yelps of pain.

'Ow! Ooch! Awww! Oh! Ooeer!' he complained as he catapulted down the lorry. On his way he uprooted the bushes and knocked over the fence.

Finally he pinged off the end of the lorry and fell in a heap of discarded soil. He lay there complaining but, as usual, unhurt.

'You pea-brained, stupid, float-wrecking idiot,' I yelled at the sad-looking Lump.

'Sorry,' he whimpered.

I turned away and looked at the damage. Actually, quite by accident, he had made the float look better. The things he had 'removed' allowed everything to be seen. With a bit of touching up everything would look just right.

It was hard to say it, but I did. 'Thanks, Lump. You've made a good job of that.'

He couldn't tell whether I was being sarcastic at first. But I think he believed me.

Sam and I had persuaded the City Council to let us borrow some waste bins. So now we had to gather some suitable litter to get us started. Mo had a good idea. We could pick up litter along the way and throw it on the float as we went along. Those on the float could then demonstrate our litter-picking skills with a constant supply. Loaded sacks could be dropped through a hole into the space under the path. It sounded good! Little did I suspect the flaw in my plan!

There was just one more thing to decide. What would we wear? Whizzer came up with the answer. Every year there was a carnival in town, organized by the West Indian Community Centre. Whizzer's mum was on the committee, and he persuaded her to let us borrow some costumes.

She came up with a set of dragon costumes. I don't know what they had to do with the environment, but they did look different, especially on Lump!

Ever since we'd seen Anne Calder in the café, Sam had been worried about the threat from the City Club. So Sparky and I volunteered to sleep by the float on the night before the Carnival to protect it. I didn't think it was really necessary, but it would be good fun.

At about half past nine Sparky and I settled down in my tent to a restless night's sleep, interrupted by a very enthusiastic Wally, my stupid guard dog. I had brought him along to warn us if someone was breaking into the yard, but he was far too excited by the adventure to be any use.

Eventually I managed to settle him down, and Sparky and I dozed off to sleep.

'What was that?' I woke with a start.

Wally had gone, and I could hear barking in the distance. Sparky and I crawled out of the tent. It was a cloudless summer night, and by the eerie light of the moon, we nervously crawled round the lorry in the general direction of the barking.

'Ssshh,' I whispered to Sparky, trying not to sound petrified, which I was. 'Let's creep up on them and see who it is.'

My knees were knocking so much, creeping was all I could do. Anyway, if they were bigger than me, I wasn't going to get myself beaten up by barging in on them or trying to capture them. In fact, I hadn't got a clue what to do if we found anyone.

We crept closer and closer to the barking. Wally was going nuts. It was coming from round the side of the building. We nervously edged closer. I found a lump of wood to defend myself with. From the noise it sounded as though I might need it.

I peeped cautiously round the wall.

The stupid animal was leaping up and down, barking like a dog gone crazy, at a pathetic black alley cat looking down from the top of a wall. All you could see was an outline and two bright eyes. That cat was just playing with our stupid animal, watching it going crazy for the fun of it. When it saw us the cat leapt away.

Wally looked satisfied at frightening it off, and turned to me expecting praise for his good work. I could feel my hand tightening on the piece of wood. I lifted it. Wally's ears went back. He knew he had done something to make me very unhappy, but hadn't got a clue what it was.

I threw the piece of wood after the cat.

'You stupid animal,' I shouted at Wally. 'Get back to the tent.' He followed the direction of my pointing finger with his tail between his legs.

It seemed as if we spent the whole night controlling that over-excited hound. By the morning both Sparky and I were exhausted and just a little bad-tempered. When the others arrived, they understood our mood from the tone of our grunts and kept their distance until we 'came round'.

After several cups of coffee, and some breakfast, my spirits were revived and I was ready to join in the fun. We had the rest of the morning to sort out the float and get it ready for the parade. Unfortunately it had rained again in the morning and made the grass on the float a bit slippy, but I still had great confidence in my plan.

Everything was ready so we all got dressed up in our dragon outfits. I was to be on the float, together with Chip, Mo, and Lump. The others were to walk alongside, gathering litter. We had decided to put Lump at the top of the path, where he could stand and wave and cause least trouble. The easiest way to get him up there was to use a ladder and help him get on directly, rather than walk up the little incline that we had built.

With all the signs we had made and the costumes, it looked quite good, even Sam had to admit that. Angelica drove the lorry and we made our way to the assembly point. The floats were to be judged when they went past the City Hall. Modest as ever, I thought we stood a good chance. But when I saw the huge float from the new factory I was a bit miffed. Sam went berserk.

'How dare they turn up with all that impressive stuff about the environment. It's not fair. If they had spent the money from the float on the environment rather than telling us a load of rubbish about what they pretend to do to help . . .' Sam's mutterings died down as all the lorries went to line up for the parade.

I looked up at Lump, high on his artificial 'hill'. He looked petrified, squeezed into his tight-fitting dragon costume, clinging on to the top of the lorry above the driver's cab. 'For goodness' sake, Lump, cheer up. You'll put everybody off,' I yelled. He let go with one arm, smiled weakly from under the dragon's teeth, and limply waved one arm.

The parade was going well. We were getting lots of cheers and claps. I thought we stood a good chance. After the next corner we would be in the market square, in front of the City Hall.

'Come on, everybody,' I yelled. 'Let's really turn it on now.'

I looked up at Lump. 'Come on, Lump,' I demanded. 'More waving. We'll have some chocolate if we win.'

I shouldn't have said that. He suddenly became very enthusiastic.

Just then I noticed some friends from school and leaned down to chat. They were two girls from the year above. Very pretty!

'Hi,' I called, leaning casually over the edge of the lorry. I thought I looked rather macho. I had forgotten that I was wearing a dragon costume. Mistaking their laughter for admiration I leaned further, lost my grip and fell from the lorry. Fortunately, Doug was in the driver's cab looking back and told Angelica to stop, which she did. Quickly!

I looked up. Lump was wobbling.

'For goodness' sake, hold on,' I shouted.

I jumped back quickly onto the lorry. What I didn't know was that Doug couldn't see Lump so he told Angelica to drive on.

We were passing the judging stand, and Lump was in maximum unstable mode. Just at that moment a well-aimed can caught him, just above the dragon's jaw. It was the final nudge.

'Whoaa,' Lump screamed, as he lost his grip and slid down our constructed sloping path. As he went down, he grabbed at one of the remaining bushes, which came away, as did most of the soil and grass, loosened by the morning rain. The whole lot slid in a slow motion landslide, picking up Mo, Chip and myself, and landed us all in a great mess at the back of the lorry. Luckily, the tailboard stopped the whole lot, including us, sliding off the back.

As I looked around I saw the horror on the rest of the gang's faces, and the smirk on the face of Anne Calder of City Club who must have lobbed the can.

Grass, soil and dragons lay in an untidy heap. I waved limply at the judges as we passed them. They looked confused. The rest of the crowd fell about laughing.

Lump looked up. 'Did we win?' he asked.

I threw the nearest grass turf at him.

6
No Such Thing as a Free Sweatshirt

'Two wins out of three wasn't bad,' Doug said sooth-ingly to the gang as we sat in the club hut recovering from the humiliation of the parade.

'Two wins out of three was great,' I responded. 'But I don't know how I'm going to face going back to school next term.'

I turned on Lump. 'It was all your fault,' I grumbled.

Sam turned on me. 'Oh no, it wasn't,' she said. 'It was all *your* fault, Nick.'

I looked at her and felt hurt. After all the work I had put into getting the thing together, how could she say that?

'You and your crackpot ideas,' she went on. 'If you hadn't insisted on that daft idea for the float we might have stood a chance. You're so frightened of losing your power as leader of the gang, that you have to bully everyone into doing what you want, whether it's right or wrong.'

She got up and walked out, slamming the door behind her. The hut shook. When Sam got angry, she really got angry. I looked round at everybody. I could see from their faces that they thought Sam was right. I decided to do what any self-respecting gang leader would do. I got up, looking angry, and left, slamming the door even harder than Sam!

But I didn't feel angry inside. Sam was right and I was stupid. I knew it really. But if I admitted that, I would look an even bigger fool! I walked slowly home wondering what to do next. As I came round the corner into our street I could see Sam sitting on the wall outside our houses looking glum. What should I do?

I decided to face the music.

'What do you want?' she grumbled as I approached.

I was going to tell her that I thought she was getting a bit over the top with all this environmental stuff. I was going to say that maybe I did do a few, a very few, things a *bit* wrong. I was going to say how hard it was to be the leader of the gang and have to get things right all the time. Instead, inspiration and the understanding that I had been a real plonker came upon me as I walked up to her.

'I'm sorry,' was all I said.

She jumped off the wall and flung her arms round me. It felt good.

I put my arms round her and we hugged each other. Suddenly I heard cheers and clapping in my ears. The rest of the gang were standing up the street! We both went very red and let go of each other quickly. I mumbled a goodnight and shuffled, embarrassed, into the house.

Saying sorry really does you good. It kind of frees up a lot of the anger bottled up inside you, and I felt much happier. I decided it was time to stop being so bossy with the gang.

Just before I went to sleep, I thought about how pigheaded I'd been. There was somebody else I had to say sorry to. Somebody who was always ready to give you another chance. 'I'm sorry, God,' I whispered.

The next day was Sunday, and in church, apart from noticing how nice Sam was looking, I listened to Doug talking about how Jesus treated his disciples, his gang. He spent his time trying to help them to be better, caring for them and encouraging them. He trained them so well that they became people who helped change thousands of other people's lives. There was a lesson for me there!

As I went out of church that morning Doug just winked at me. I grinned sheepishly. It was great to be friends again with my mates. As for Doug, he'd never let me down.

The next day we were going on the trip round Rawson Marsden—part of the prize in the music competition. I couldn't wait to see how far Sam got round the visit before exploding. I was rather relieved to see Doug was going as well. We met at the club hut.

'Now, for goodness' sake, let's not have any trouble today,' he begged.

'Trouble? Us? What do you mean?' I responded on behalf of the gang. As if we would ever get into any bother!

At the factory gate we were met by a man in uniform. He looked as if he had just come from beating up somebody. He was big, hard and mean-looking. He marched us to a building on one side of the factory which contained offices, and we were shown into a large posh room with a big table and leather chairs.

'This is the boardroom,' Doug said.

I didn't see any boards, only the gang who were 'bored'! After a while, in marched Mr Brown, the boss. Behind him were two ladies dressed in green sweatshirts with *Rawson Marsden Cares For The Environment* written across them in large letters. And behind them came a bloke from the local newspaper with a camera. It was a set-up.

We were all given sweatshirts, and before we knew what was happening, found ourselves standing round Mr Brown, hemmed in by the two over-made-up ladies, grinning peculiarly and giving a stupid thumbs-up sign.

'One more. Keep smiling,' the pressman whined. 'Now come on, little lady, join in,' he added to the fuming Sam.

She reluctantly gave in. It was the only way to get away from the horrible, pushy group of people.

'I'll give you the words later,' Mr Brown said to the man from the press, then to us, 'I'll send someone to show you round,' and with that he disappeared with the two ladies.

The pressman took all our names, then left, and we were left sitting there, drinking the orange juice provided and chewing on the biscuits.

Sam ignored the biscuits. She was fuming. I avoided even looking at her.

A young woman came in. 'All right, lovies?' she trilled.

I took an instant dislike to her.

'I'm going to show you round the factory,' she went on patronisingly. 'Now, don't you touch anything unless I say so, and don't ask me any awkward questions—I'm not a scientist, you know.'

First of all she sat us down in the plush leather chairs and switched on a slide show. Yawn! I felt like going to sleep. It was all about the factory and how wonderful it was. As soon as it was finished, Sam started. The lady had asked us to call her Sandra.

'Excuse me, Sandra,' Sam began politely enough, 'In the slide show it talked a lot about the environment and what the company was doing for it. We also saw a wonderful float at the parade. Could you tell us exactly how much money the firm actually spends on the environment compared with how much it spends *telling* people about the environment?'

Sam was clever, but I suspect that someone like Angelica had put her up to this. Doug looked blank. Sandra looked even blanker.

'Thank you for that interesting question, dearie,' she responded weakly. 'I don't have the figures, but I'm sure that this company, which is proud of its work on the environment, does a great deal.' She fumbled around with her papers and handed Sam a glossy leaflet—to try and shut her up, of course.

Before Sam could return to the attack, we were

hustled out of the room and on to the yard where we were all handed hard hats. Whizzer in particular found this difficult, trying every way possible to squeeze his shock of black hair and his stereo headphones under the bright yellow plastic. We all looked silly.

Sandra waved her arm round the yard, showing us where the lorries came in with materials to make the plastic containers, metals for the tin cans and chemicals. The plant made metal and plastic containers, and filled some of them. She also showed us where the lorries went out with their loads of finished containers. All pretty boring so far. I knew that because Lump had started to eat, Whizzer was lost in his music, and Chip was playing a computer game.

Sandra had great difficulty in pulling us all together before we began a tour of the inside of the factory. She also handed out ear muffs for the noisy bits. She didn't bother with Whizzer. In the first bit they were making large biscuit tins. Plates of sheet metal were punched on a big machine and the cutouts were then moulded by another machine. Operators fed them through the different machines very quickly, until at the end of the line, biscuit tins appeared at great speed. I wouldn't have been so bored if there had actually been some biscuits in them.

Then we saw a machine which made metal cigar containers. This was great. A little round blank was put into the machine and compressed air was fired at it, forcing it into a mould, and that was all there was to it. It was great. We all had a go, or at least, we were allowed to press the button and to take away our efforts.

The next building had rows of production lines with metal cans rattling along, millions of them, at great speed. I didn't know how anyone could work with all that noise. The only one not bothered by it was Whizzer, who was moving to the sound of the music in his headphones.

As we moved along the lines of tins, our guide pointed at things but we couldn't hear a word she said. It seemed like my idea of hell, and I made a mental note that that was one job I wouldn't do when I left school.

Meanwhile, Chip had become fascinated by the control panel for one of the production lines. It was full of switches and lights. Sandra read his mind. She wagged her finger at him and shook her head. He got the message.

However, neither of them had allowed for Whizzer. While Sandra explained to Chip what he shouldn't do, we all stopped in the narrow passage between two rows of machines. Whizzer was totally unaware of what was happening—on another planet! With fingers clicking and hips swaying he ploughed into our cramped group.

At that moment, Sandra's finger was pointing at a row of switches. As body cannoned off body, the inevitable happened. She was pushed and her finger hit the panel. That part of the production line stopped and the rest kept going. Cans started crunching up, and then began to fall off the line, then fly off like mortars in a battle. An engineer rushed up and threw a switch, stopping the lot. You should have seen Sandra's face! I tried hard not to laugh. She shooed us away quickly, climbing over a pile of tins.

We were hustled into another building where plastic bottles were made in moulds. It was much quieter.

'Don't touch *anything*,' Sandra commanded in a harassed voice. I had the feeling that she just wanted to get this tour over with as quickly as possible. From then on she moved us round the building at great speed.

'Any questions?' Sandra trilled after another boring description of what went on. She obviously hadn't a clue really, but had just memorized the script. So far, nobody had asked anything, and she was not expecting anything now. She was already on the move when Sam piped up.

'What happens to all the waste from the factory?' she asked.

Sandra was ready for this. She went in to a long and boring speech about tankers taking it away to be dealt with.

'All of it?' Sam went on.

'Why, of course, my dear,' said Sandra with a patronizing smile.

'Where do those pipes go then?' Sam pointed to two pipes going through the wall of the factory from a tank in the corner of the room.

'They go into the larger storage tank,' Sandra responded.

'How can they?' Sam asked. 'I've looked out of the window and the canal is just outside.'

Sandra was getting flustered. 'I'm sure you're wrong, dear, Rawson Marsden do not do things like that. Come along now, let's get on.' And she hustled us away.

We were quickly moved on and before we knew it we were out of the factory with the briefest of goodbyes. I think Sandra had had enough.

As we left she gave us each a carrier bag of bits and pieces, all with RAWSON MARSDEN on them. I like freebies and started digging around to see what we had been given—a pen, a badge, some plastic containers . . .

'Great—sweets!' Lump shouted, and we all dug down to find them in our bags.

All except Sam, who threw her bag down in disgust.

'Whatever's up with you?' I asked.

'Don't you see what they're doing?' she rounded on me.

'Oh come on, Sam, give it a rest. Let's just enjoy the freebies,' I responded.

'Sometimes, Nick Baker,' she said angrily, 'you're just a stupid little twerp.'

She hauled off the free sweatshirt and threw it to the floor, kicked the bag of freebies into the middle of the road, and stormed off!

7

Nick & Co. Take Action

We sat quietly in the club hut. Everyone was steering clear of Sam, who was still in an awful mood after the previous day's trip to the factory. When Mo attempted to give her back the sweatshirt and bag of goodies which she had thrown away, they disappeared out of the window.

'Right, folks,' I said, trying to break the ice, 'I'm getting bored sitting around. Let's get some games going.'

Everybody set to with pool, table tennis, darts, table football. That is, everyone except Sam. She slumped in one of the easy chairs with her head in her hands. Suddenly she got up, scowled at everybody, and left, slamming the door so hard the whole hut shook!

That was *my* trick—and the second time she'd done it in a week. We all looked at each other. I decided I had better do something, so I went after Sam. I didn't have far to go. She was sitting on the step outside. I sat down beside her.

There was a long silence.

'You're all so two-faced,' Sam eventually said. 'After all the work we put into the parade, and all that was said in the music competition, nobody stood up to that factory. All you could do was sit there and accept some little toys, just because they were free. You make me sick.'

Of course she was right. But I didn't think the way she was going about telling us was particularly right. I didn't quite know how to tell her, because of my long history of unreasonableness and door slamming. In the end, I didn't have to say anything.

After another long silence, Sam spoke.

'All right, I know,' she went on. 'Sorry. I shouldn't have slammed the door. I shouldn't have lost my temper.'

I didn't know what to do and as nobody was watching I put my arm round her. I think that helped.

After a while she sighed heavily and stood up. 'I was wrong in my attitude,' she said firmly. 'But right about what I saw.'

'Oh, no,' I groaned.

We went back into the hut and Sam asked everyone to stop what they were doing and listen. She apologized, then she set about suggesting a plan.

'I think we should go back and investigate the pipes I saw,' she said. 'I'm *sure* they're dumping stuff straight into the canal.'

The gang murmured a bit, which generally meant that they thought it was a reasonable idea. I wasn't so sure, but it did sound like fun, and even a bit exciting, so I was willing to give it a go. After all, it was about time Nick & Co. saw some action. Things were a bit flat after all the excitement of the raft race and the music competition. Though I still blushed when I thought about the float.

So Sam outlined a plan for us to return to the canal the next day.

We met outside our house, so that Doug wouldn't find out and try to stop us. It was some time since I had been to this stretch of the canal opposite the new factory. The towpath was closed off—with a high wire fence. As Sparky investigated the fence, the rest of us looked up the canal towards the factory. On the opposite bank the large wall of the new factory towered over the water. It was impossible to see very far because the canal curved. We *had* to get past the fence.

Sparky came back and then led us a little way along the fence to a spot where it was pushed up a bit, and the earth had been scooped away underneath.

'I found this spot and made it bigger so that we could all get through,' Sparky said, looking pointedly at Lump.

We all climbed through except Lump, who managed to get stuck and make an awful lot of noise as we pushed and pulled him through. I was glad not to be him, not least because he was already smeared with mud from the tight squeeze under the fence. His mother would not be pleased!

On the other side of the fence the bank was very overgrown and we had to fight through to the edge of the canal and the towpath. As we rounded the curve in the canal we could see an old shed with a narrow boat moored alongside. Sam and I led the way and we edged carefully along, not knowing what to expect. So far we hadn't seen any sign of those pipes, but Sam reckoned that they were further down the canal.

There was loads of noise coming from the factory, but our side of the canal was strangely quiet and eerie. I didn't like it. It made me jumpy.

Whizzer was wandering along at the back as usual, plugged into his Walkman. He didn't notice a step in the path and there was a sudden blast of music as he tripped and dropped his personal stereo, pulling the headphone lead out and letting us all get a blast of his favourite music.

I nearly jumped out of my skin. 'Whizzer,' I hissed through clenched teeth.

'Sorry, man,' he replied, 'It was an accident.' He picked it up and plugged himself back in again.

'Be careful,' I went on, but there was no point. He couldn't hear a thing.

Meanwhile Wally had been as good as gold. I hadn't particularly wanted to take the daft thing along, but walking the dog had been a good excuse for going out. Well, Wally was definitely 'three prawns short of a seafood salad' when it came to brains, but so far he had got the message of being quiet and obedient. The sudden music must have stirred up his limited number of brain cells. He suddenly shot off into the undergrowth, barking and yelping for all he was worth. It wasn't long before he reappeared further down the towpath, only by then he wasn't alone. He was heading back fast in our direction, chased by a small but very aggressive duck.

We all fell about laughing, but not for long. Behind the duck came something, somebody else. A strange man was running along the path. 'Stop! Stop!' he was yelling.

He had very long, bushy hair, a beard, and a strange selection of brightly-coloured clothes on. I didn't like the look of this.

'Run for it!' I yelled.

The gang did not need telling twice. We all turned on our heels and hurtled back towards the fence. I wasn't quite sure how we were all going to get back through the hole. It was bad enough running along the towpath, barging into each other, and complaining about the slower ones getting in the way.

We all arrived at the fence almost together. A good leader would have organized the troops at this stage, but just then I didn't want to be a good leader, and none of the others looked keen to take on the role. It was a case of personal survival!

Sparky and Raj reached the hole first, diving through the undergrowth and the hole in the fence in almost one movement. Sam followed, and then I pushed my little sister Mo through and clambered after her. By then Raj and Sparky were shouting encouragement from the safe side, and Lump and Chip were shouting in fear from behind.

When I made it through I looked round. Lump was starting to force his way through the gap.

'Hurry up!' yelled a panicking Chip.

'Come on, come on,' Raj and Sparky shouted, as they tried to drag Lump through.

Lump was snagged up on the fence. Of course, when you are in a panic, you don't slow down to sort things out, you speed up and get in an even bigger tangle. At least, that's what Lump did. The more everyone shouted and the more he struggled, the more jammed he became.

I could hear the duck squawking, Wally barking and the man shouting, all getting nearer.

Chip just couldn't wait for Lump. He decided to go a different route. He started to climb the fence, using overhanging trees to help. Chip is not a great climber. The fence was a bit wobbly and some old bits of wire stuck out of it.

I have never seen Chip climb so quickly. But the snags of wire and tree branches snatched at his clothing and things started to come out of his pockets—his precious computer games, assorted bits of electronic equipment, bits of wire, screwdrivers, etc, etc. At last Lump was dragged through the fence and Chip fell in a crumpled heap by his side.

Wally was getting closer, but where was Whizzer? SPERLASH!! We got the answer. He had got behind, trying to sort out his earphones. Coming to the fence he saw the log-jam at the hole, so he took the only route left. The canal!

We gathered together on the other side of the fence, scratched, bedraggled heaps. Just then Wally hurtled up beside us, leaving the angry duck on the other side of the fence.

The strange man was running along the towpath shouting something like 'What, what?' It didn't make sense, but we didn't wait to find out what he was really saying. We ran off together along the path and back home. When we reached the road I looked back. The man had picked up the duck and was looking in our direction. He waved.

Weird!

As we reached the end of our street I looked at us all. We were in a real mess. Whizzer was soaked to the skin and desperately trying to dry out his Walkman, Sparky and Chip were covered in scratches from the wire and had torn their clothes. The rest of us didn't look much better, all covered in dirt.

There was a general nervousness in the air as we all thought of how we were going to face our parents. We were all wondering if there was any chance of sneaking into our respective houses and cleaning up before we were found out.

'OK,' I said, attempting to be brave about it all. 'We'll meet in the club in a couple of hours. Those that make it through the parent barrier, that is.'

Nobody laughed.

Mo and I tried to sneak into the house without being seen, but Wally gave the game away. As soon as he was in the door, he had to find Mum to give her a friendly hello bark. She was immediately suspicious, and caught us halfway up the stairs.

'Back!' she called.

We stood in the kitchen, heads bowed, as Mum

gave us a fearful telling off. Boy, did we have to pay. We had to wash all our own clothes, and tidy our rooms. That was a bit much! By the time I made it to the club it was really late.

Nobody else had made it. Only Doug sat there, drumming his fingers.

'Where *is* everybody?' he demanded.

Before I had chance to reply he launched into a real moan about the mess in the club hut. How we all talked about the environment and yet let the place become an absolute pigsty. He went on and on and on.

I couldn't take any more. Rather than attempting to argue, I just turned round and walked out.

8
Eric and Walter the Duck

'Nick! Get up!' Mum's voice echoed up the stairs.

My bed was so warm and cosy that I often found it impossible to move in the morning, and I had to be 'persuaded'. Mum was good at persuading! I heard the click of the door, and felt a sudden cold draught of air as the covers were whisked from the bed.

'Come on, Rip Van Winkle,' Mum went on. 'Get out of this festering pit and *do* something.'

It was the holidays and I couldn't see any reason why I had to get up. Mum was probably jealous because she had to work while I enjoyed my warm bed. I said that to Mum and it didn't go down too well! After yet another 'ear-wigging' from her, I got up, had breakfast and escaped to sit on the wall outside our house, kicking my heels.

After all the excitement of the City Festival, there was nothing to do. This was going to be a long, boring holiday. I couldn't spend the entire time on the front wall, but every time I went in the house I had to *do* something—clean my room, wash the dishes, run an errand, clean my shoes—the list was endless.

I decided I needed to keep myself as busy as possible, doing the things I wanted to do, only coming home for food and sleep as necessary, but at the same time keeping Mum and Dad happy. I wasn't sure this was humanly possible!

After a while Sam came out from her house to join me. She didn't have to say anything, but I knew she was feeling the same things. We sat on the wall for ages without saying anything. I was thinking about the excitement of the day before. I liked an adventure. I wasn't really totally convinced about all this environmental stuff, but it had all the makings of a good adventure!

'Sam,' I said eventually. 'What about another nose around the canal? Without Wally and the rest of the gang this time.'

'Well,' Sam replied, 'if you hadn't suggested it in another five minutes, I was going to go on my own.'

I laughed. Without another word, we jumped off the wall and made our way back to the canal. The hole in the fence was now quite big enough—Lump had made sure of that yesterday—and so we had no difficulty in getting through without dirtying our clothes. Very cautiously we looked down the towpath to see if it was clear. Nobody was about.

We edged down the path, keeping close to the bushes where we could hide quickly if anyone came along. Working our way along we came round the curve and saw again the old hut and also the narrow boat moored alongside. There was still nobody about.

We carried on, creeping very carefully so as not to cause any noise or disturbance.

When we reached the wall near the narrow boat we stopped.

The boat was beautifully painted and cared for, with pots of flowers and polished pieces of equipment. What spoilt its beauty was the sight of the ugly new factory behind it.

'What do we do now?' I whispered to Sam.

'Let's have a closer look at the boat,' she whispered back. 'It doesn't look as if anyone's around.'

'Why are we whispering then?' I whispered back.

'I don't know,' she whispered in return.

We looked at each other and burst out laughing.

Walking over to the boat I started looking through the windows. Inside it was like a perfect little house, with a small cooker, a tiny dining area, a neat little sleeping area, and another sort of sitting area. Everything was spotlessly neat and tidy, but with lots of bits of wood carving lying around. There were also other things which my mum calls 'knick-knacks' filling all the shelves and the tops of the furniture. It looked really interesting.

At the back was an area with a steering wheel and the engine controls. I climbed up and pretended to drive the boat, making engine noises, as if I was Nigel Mansell, which was a bit silly on a narrow boat. Sam was not impressed.

She started off down the towpath a little further. She was determined to find out where those factory pipes came out. Suddenly Sam turned back and ran towards me, pointing across the canal.

'There,' she said. 'I knew it. Look.'

I followed her pointing finger and saw two pipes coming out of the factory and disappearing into the water. They were difficult to see, quite small like water pipes, and had been well hidden.

'Oh come on, Sam, they're just little pipes. They don't mean anything,' I said. I was more interested in exploring the boat. I jumped on board and looked down the length of the boat through the hatch.

'I don't think you should do that,' Sam said.

I didn't get a chance to continue my investigation.

'Quack!'

In the distance we heard the unmistakeable cry of the demented duck which had caused all the problems yesterday.

'Quick, behind the wall,' I whispered, and we dived for cover. We were just in time, as the strange man came round the corner, preceded by his feathered friend. Sam was about to say something, but I put my finger to my mouth, and we both tucked down tightly behind the wall. The man and the duck arrived at the boat. I heard him climb on board and drop down the ramp for his duck.

'Looks like we've had visitors,' the man said.

I had opened the hatch a little way and hadn't had time to slide it back.

The duck started quacking furiously.

'What's the matter?' the man asked. 'Where are you going?' I heard the quacking of the duck getting nearer. Suddenly, round the wall came the aggressive little beast. Obviously a tracker duck!

We stood up and backed away.

The man was close behind, holding a lump of wood. He looked at us and seemed relieved. Quickly he dropped the wood.

'OK, Walter,' he called to the demented duck. 'Well done, but I don't think these two are going to harm us.'

The duck calmed down.

'You'd better come out from there,' he said to us. 'Don't worry, we're not going to hurt you.'

His calm manner reassured us, and we climbed out onto the towpath. He looked at us and the duck flapped its wings, ready to launch at us if we tried anything.

'Aren't you the ones I saw yesterday?' he asked.

We didn't answer.

We had only seen him from a distance, and up close, he looked even stranger than we had thought. It wasn't that he was like a tramp, because he wasn't dirty or anything, but his clothes weren't the sort of things you saw every day in the High Street. He was wearing a sort of thin shirt in bright colours, and jeans with a brightly decorated patch over one knee. Instead of socks and shoes he wore clogs.

Tied round his neck was a brightly-coloured neckerchief, but you couldn't see a lot of it because of the large bushy beard which seemed to cover most of his face and chest. It was as if his hair had all slipped off his head onto his face, because there wasn't much 'on top', just long streaky bits down the side, and the rest tied at the back. Out of this mass of hair peered two searching eyes. Was this a real hippie? Somebody even weirder than Angelica?

Sam broke the silence. 'We're here because we're very worried about the pollution of the canal,' she said firmly.

I nodded wisely and left the talking to her.

'What we're trying to do is find out where the pollution is coming from,' she went on.

'I see,' the man replied. 'And you think I may have something to do with it?'

'No, no,' Sam said quickly. 'I'm sure it's the factory over there that's doing it.' She went on to describe our visit to the factory and what we had seen. He got the full lecture on the environment, together with bits from our science lessons. Once Sam got going I thought she was never going to stop. The man just nodded and listened.

And when Sam had run out of steam he introduced himself.

'I'm Eric,' he said. 'And this is my guard duck, Walter.'

He pointed to the duck, who responded with an aggressive 'QUACK'. I stepped back.

'Oh, don't worry,' Eric went on. 'His quack is worse than his peck, if you see what I mean.'

We laughed and Walter fluttered his feathers. It seemed uncanny how much he understood of the conversation. I think it had something to do with the way you say things.

'I think that your concern for the environment is terrific,' Eric continued. 'But I think this particular cause is one that you should leave well alone.'

'Why?' demanded Sam.

'I'm sure there are other things that you could pursue, litter on the streets, mess in the park,' he went on, not directly answering Sam's question.

Sam wouldn't let him get away with that. 'You're just putting us down because we're kids. Grown-ups are always doing that,' she grumbled. 'I'm fed up with it. It's the grown-ups that have got this world into the mess it's in. If they had done something about that factory when it was built, we wouldn't have to be doing this.' She was getting cross, and Walter was getting edgy. I backed away further, not wanting chewed ankles.

'What about those pipes down there?' she demanded, pointing in the direction of her investigations. 'When we visited the factory I saw some pipes leaving the building that could only go to the canal. Now I can see what I think are the same pipes disappearing into the canal, and we all know the canal is polluted further down.'

Eric just listened calmly. 'Look,' he said, 'It's great that you care about the environment. But, for a start, the pollution doesn't start where those pipes enter the canal, but from the people developing the products. And secondly, this is something that is far too serious for you to get involved.'

'What do you mean?' I asked.

'I don't mean anything,' he answered—'that is of interest to you.'

There was a silence. He was obviously not telling us something.

'I think you should go,' he suddenly said.

In spite of Sam's protests he led us up a path away from the canal, which came out, surprisingly for us, quite near Angelica's workshop. As he pushed us out of the small gate and on to the road, he told us not to come back. He wasn't unfriendly, but obviously he didn't want to talk about things.

Sam was furious and grumbled all the way home. I knew this wasn't going to be the end of it.

9
Sam Goes Bananas

As we walked away from the canal, Sam was so mad I could almost see the steam coming out of her ears. There was no way that she was going to let this thing drop. It was a bit like Wally with his favourite bone. The harder you tried to get it away from him, the tighter he gripped it with his teeth and the louder his growls. Sam was surely growling, and each time someone said stop, the more determined she was not to stop.

I suggested that we call in on Angelica. I thought that maybe she could reason with Sam. But Sam just walked past Angelica's with no answer. We got all the way home and she still hadn't spoken, but her face was a picture of fury. Back outside our houses we sat on our favourite wall again. My dad reckoned there was a groove where we had kicked our heels for so long. I knew we wouldn't be sitting for long this time because Sam had a wild look in her eyes. It was like sitting next to a volcano about to erupt!

'Wait here!' she demanded suddenly.

I didn't argue. The door slammed and everything

went quiet. Soon the door opened and out she came, slamming the door again, and carrying a plastic carrier bag.

'What's in there?' I asked nervously.

She opened it up. Inside were the sweatshirt and other things given to her on the visit to the factory. She had never worn them, and only had them at all because Sparky rescued them from the middle of the road where she had kicked them.

'Get yours,' she demanded.

'Why?' I responded weakly.

'Just get them,' she replied.

I thought it best to go along and humour her, so I went to my house and dug out the sweatshirt I had been given. I had made a real effort to tidy up my room and it looked good provided nobody looked too closely behind cupboard doors. OK, I had given in, but it was either that or not eating.

The sweatshirt was already messed up and torn, and I had to retrieve it from the back of the drawer where I had hidden it from my mum. I had already lost most of the other things I had been given. I thought Sam was going to do something like throwing them in the dustbin, and I was happy to go along with that because the sweatshirt was no use anyway, but I was wrong.

I met up with Sam back on the street. She had a steely look in her eye. 'Right, follow me,' she demanded.

'Where are we going?' I asked.

'Back to that stinking factory to throw these grotty

things in their stupid faces!' she said coldly.

This did not seem a good idea, even to me. I was the last person to hold back when I had a 'bee in my bonnet' about something, but I had been learning that it wasn't always the best thing to do something without thinking, even if it *seemed* the best thing to do! I could feel in my bones that this was going to lead to big trouble. I could see the scene now with my dad. It's not easy having a policeman for a dad. I shuddered. I couldn't let Sam go through this on her own—maybe I could do something to stop her.

'Er, Sam, are you sure about this?' I asked breathlessly, trying to keep up at a fast walk alongside her.

She stopped sharply, and I skidded to a halt at her side. She turned to face me, still with the steely look in her eye.

'This has got to be done,' she insisted. 'Are you with me or against me?'

I nodded weakly.

On the way we met Mo and Sparky, who insisted on coming too. I didn't want them to get involved in what I knew was going to be a disaster, but they wouldn't be put off. Maybe the three of us could sit on Sam till she calmed down, but I doubted it.

The walk to the factory was like a dream—or was it a nightmare?—with Sam marching ahead and the rest of us trying to slow things down with no success. We reached the gates of the factory in double-quick time, and stopped a little way off. By the gates was the huge, ugly security guard, doing a good imitation of the Incredible Hulk! How were we going to get past him?

'What we need is some kind of diversion,' Sam observed. I was hoping that we couldn't think of one and I could change Sam's mind while we waited. No chance! Tripping across the yard came the very same Sandra who had shown us round.

The Hulk wandered over to chat to her. At that moment a lorry came along the road and slowly began to turn into the factory yard, stopping at the barrier.

'Come on,' Sam demanded, and we sprinted to the far side of the lorry, away from the Hulk. He came back to let the lorry in, and we walked alongside as it slowly entered the yard, using it to hide behind.

As soon as we got near the offices we made a dash for their doors, hoping that nobody was watching. Fortunately Sandra had continued her chat with Monster Man, and we made it to relative safety. What now?

Following Sam we leapt through a side door, and down a long corridor to the room where we had first met the manager, Mr Brown. We could hear voices the other side of the big doors. Before I could stop her, Sam burst through the doors, straight into a meeting between Mr Brown and the Mayor. I recognized him immediately. *Oh no!* I groaned to myself. Sam didn't stop. She threw the bag of goodies on to the table.

'I'm returning these,' she said to the astounded man. 'I don't want anything from a company that says one thing and does another. You are polluting the canal with your waste and you shouldn't be allowed to carry on.'

She turned to us. I sheepishly put my bagful on the

table and we all nodded in agreement.

Mr Brown was very red-faced. He picked up the phone and shouted into it, 'Get Hargreaves and Sandra here now—immediately!' Then he turned on us. 'How dare you break into my factory and disturb this very important meeting I'm having with the Mayor. What on earth do you think you are doing?' he demanded.

'How dare you pollute our city?' Sam responded. 'And why are you letting him?' she demanded, turning on the Mayor.

'What are you talking about?' Mr Brown shouted. Everyone was getting hysterical.

'What about the pipe...?' Sam began, only to be cut short by the appearance of a very red-faced Sandra and a furious Hargreaves.

'Get these young hooligans off these premises *now*,' Mr Brown demanded. 'And I'll see you both later!'

We were bundled roughly out of the room.

'I know who you are, and I'll be seeing those responsible for you,' was Mr Brown's parting shot as he slammed his door.

Before Sam could respond, Hargreaves the Hulk grabbed her and pulled her away. This I was not going to have. Without thinking I kicked him hard on the leg. He yelled in pain and turned on me. 'Why, you little...' He never finished the sentence. Just at that moment more of the factory people came along and grabbed us. Hargreaves took great delight in dragging me down the stairs. He was holding me so tightly I thought I would burst.

We were thrown out of the main entrance on to the

path. Sandra never said a word, but Hargreaves looked very mean. If there had not been some of the factory workers and drivers about I think he would have been far worse.

'I'll not forget you. So watch out,' he hissed at us as he turned and walked back into the factory yard.

I only just managed to stop Sam going back in. I was pretty mad by now, but even fearless Nick Baker knew when to make a tactical retreat!

'I'm still going to do something about this,' she insisted. But my only thoughts were about how we were going to avoid our parents getting to know about it. As we walked back home, Sam came up with a new idea every five yards. I decided it was time to change the subject. After all, I felt a bit responsible for what had happened. I should have stopped her. But could I have?

'I have a miraculous treat for you all,' I announced. 'A true Wonder of the World. The grand opening of Nick Baker's new, improved, environmentally-friendly, super-neat bedroom.'

Sparky laughed, Mo groaned. Sam didn't even hear what I said. But they all filed into my house and up to my room to see the sight.

I opened the door with a theatrical 'Ta-da'. It did look grand. Not at all like the homely, scruffy dump that I loved and had made my own. There were no deliciously smelly clothes lying about. There were no piles of sweet wrappers and crisp bags. There were no old hairy lumps of chewing-gum to get stuck to the bottom of your feet. There were no interesting piles of junk to make things with. There were no discarded paper aeroplanes made from homework exercise papers. All the surfaces were clear. Books were stacked neatly. The floor was clear.

Sparky stood with his mouth open.

Sam just looked around and said, 'Not bad,' in a distracted sort of way.

'I don't believe this,' Sparky groaned. 'Don't let my mum see this or I'll be locked away for months to do the same.'

I had forgotten Mo, my trusty sister. She knew me too well! She grunted, walked over to my wardrobe, and opened the door.

It was like Niagara Falls. A torrent of sports equipment, shoes, clothes, and other unmentionable items fell out and completely engulfed Mo. The torrent stopped.

I shrugged my shoulders. 'Ah well,' I said, 'you can't win 'em all.'

Everyone collapsed laughing, and started throwing my dirty laundry about.

It was nice to see Sam happy again. But it didn't last for long.

'Nick!' Mum called from downstairs, 'Doug's here, and he wants to see you all *right now*.'

My stomach lurched. Sam looked furious. Sparky and Mo went pale. We filed downstairs. Doug was looking very upset.

'What have you been up to now?' Mum demanded.

'I've just had Mr Brown of Rawson Marsden on the phone,' Doug began. 'And if you don't all apologize and promise to stop making a fuss over the factory he will withdraw the money for the church hall. The Mayor is also furious at being embarrassed and is demanding an apology.'

'Oh, Nick,' Mum groaned. 'What have you done?'

'It wasn't Nick,' Sam butted in. 'It was my idea.' She went on to explain all about the pipes and the canal, and how everybody's attitudes were wrong. Just because Rawson Marsden were spraying money about didn't mean they actually did what they claimed to do, she said.

Doug listened. I could see he was very upset, but he did listen to what Sam had to say. And she put forward her case clearly, for once.

'Are you sure you did the right thing?' Doug asked when Sam had finished.

'Yes,' insisted Sam, looking angry again.

'You do realize that if you carry on, the church will lose a lot of money for the new church hall?' he went on.

'You're more worried about the money than about doing the right thing,' Sam said angrily, and she turned and ran out of the front door, crying. She slammed it with an almighty BANG. The house shook!

Doug left, white-faced and obviously upset. So did Sparky. 'See you,' he said, quietly. Mo and Mum melted away too.

When Dad got home I got a fearful telling-off and was banished to my room. When I opened my window I could hear Sam crying next door.

In my room I had time to think. I knew I had been a

coward. Sam shouldn't have been rude—even if she was right. But I wasn't in the clear either. Time to have a chat with God.

If only Doug would help us, instead of ignoring it all. Perhaps he *would* help. Perhaps Sam needed to wait a bit now she had had her say.

I started to write a letter of apology, like Doug had said. And I decided that I would listen carefully to Sam—but next time she got a mad idea, I'd stop her.

10
The Incredible Hulk
Gets Heavy

The next morning I went round to call for Sam but she was already out.

'Gone off to see some friend of Doug's,' her mum said. 'Angelica somebody or other.'

I groaned. Sam's mum looked worried. 'She is all right, isn't she?' Sam's mum asked, suddenly worried. Obviously Sam hadn't told her about the trouble at the factory, and I wasn't getting involved in that. She would find out soon enough.

'Yes,' I replied innocently. 'I'll just er . . . go on to meet her.'

I backed out of the house quickly before I was asked any more awkward questions. I didn't particularly want to go to Angelica's, she was a bit too 'patched dungarees and natural yoghurt' for me. But I didn't want Sam getting even more carried away with it all.

When I reached the woodyard, I felt a bit as if I wasn't wanted. Sam and Angelica stopped talking straight away and their faces showed that they had agreed something and didn't want to tell me what it was.

'Why don't you both go back and have another chat with Eric?' Angelica said, breaking the silence. 'He's very interesting. He was a teacher until one day he decided he'd had enough and walked out. He had just enough money to buy his narrow boat, and has lived off his wits ever since.' I wasn't that keen, but Sam insisted.

'I'll have a chat with Doug,' Angelica said to Sam, as Sam pushed me out of the yard.

'Thanks,' replied Sam.

'What was that about?' I demanded.

'Nothing for you to worry about,' she replied. Grief, she sounded like my mother. I suspected that Doug was being worked on about something. The poor bloke wouldn't stand a chance.

Sam pushed me down the street and we went down the path to the canal where Eric and Walter the duck hung out. I wasn't that keen to renew my acquaintance with that demented duck, but there was no arguing with Sam. Eric was in the boat and Sam called a greeting.

'Hello!' Eric responded hesitantly. Walter eyed me suspiciously, and gave a warning 'quack.' One false move and he had a peck at the ready.

'What brings you back?' Eric asked.

'Oh, we just wanted to get to know more about your narrow boat,' Sam said. 'Angelica said you wouldn't mind.'

'So you know Angelica. Why didn't you say before? Come aboard!' Eric said, suddenly warming to us. Anybody would think it was the *Queen Mary*! 'I thought you were just nosy kids out to make a nuisance of yourselves,' he said, looking pointedly at me!

I bristled.

Sam explained to Eric about her interest in all that environmental stuff, and he looked very impressed. This was getting boring. Then things got better. He showed us round the boat. It was very narrow, but it was amazing how much was packed into such a small space. It even had a toilet and a shower!

There was a very neat bedroom, with a real sailor's bunk-bed that Eric had bought from a shipyard. Next to that was a sort of kitchen and dining area, and then another room filled with a bench and lots of wood carvings, all at different stages of being made.

'Do you like them?' Eric asked as I picked up the carvings. Those nearly finished were rounded and smooth, and felt very comforting and nice, but I wasn't sure what they were meant to be.

'Yes,' I replied politely.

'They're lovely,' Sam added with much more enthusiasm. I thought that was a bit much. I reckoned I could have done as well and made a mental note to suggest to our craft teacher that we try it at school. If this guy could make money at it, why couldn't I?

'Where do you sell them?' Sam asked.

'At craft fairs and exhibitions,' he replied.

'Do you make a lot of money out of it?' I asked cheekily, then winced as Sam gave me a kick on the ankles.

'Hardly,' Eric replied. 'But it helps make up for the

fact that I can't start up the narrow boat repair shop I was hoping to begin here. The boats don't come here now, and I'll be following them if people have their way.'

'What do you mean?' Sam asked.

'Well, you're not the only people having trouble with that factory,' he said, jerking a thumb in its direction. 'They're trying to, shall we say, buy me out.'

'Will they win?' Sam persisted.

'Let's talk about something else,' Eric changed the subject. 'What about some of my home-made lemonade?'

He poured out some glasses of the cloudy liquid, which tasted like no lemonade I had ever had before. It was fantastic.

I was looking into my empty glass, trying to angle another drink when Walter interrupted. He had accepted our presence and been sleeping peacefully in the corner, with just a hint of a duck snore. Suddenly he leapt up, quacked, and waddled out. I thought he might have gone off for a walk or something, going about his duck's business! But he wasn't.

He started quacking loudly and insistently.

'You'd better wait here while I go and investigate,' Eric said. He left us and jumped onto the bank.

As we looked through the small windows, we saw two big men approaching, with Walter flapping furiously in front of them. One of them kicked out at Walter, missing and getting a peck on the ankle for his trouble. The other one picked up a piece of wood and was just about to wallop Walter when Eric shouted.

'Come here, Walter,' he ordered, and the duck immediately obeyed.

'Can I help you?' Eric asked politely.

'You know why we're here,' one of the men stated gruffly.

I recognized the voice. It was Hargreaves, the Incredible Hulk from the factory.

'I am *not* signing any papers,' Eric insisted.

They came up close to him, threateningly. I decided to go and help. Sam grabbed my arm and the lemonade glass tumbled to the floor. The men looked and saw our faces peering from the boat. I guess it stopped them from hitting Eric, or worse.

'Don't delay,' they said to Eric. 'You might really regret it if you do.' With that they turned and marched off.

Walter gave a sharp 'quack', and one of the men threw the piece of wood at him. It missed, but Walter could contain himself no longer. He chased after them, and their dignified exit changed to a stupid hop and run, as a very angry Walter snapped at their ankles.

Eric thanked us for being there and then insisted that it was time we left.

'But we want to help,' insisted Sam.

'You're not involved in this, and I don't want you to be,' said Eric firmly. He steered us towards the door. 'And by the way,' he said, 'if I were you, I wouldn't hang about on the towpath. Cheers!' And he watched us as we walked back up towards the road.

But we were involved. Sam was heavily into this environmental thing, and I had the smell of a good adventure in my nostrils. We talked all the way back to the club hut about things and then told the gang what Eric had said. I thought we ought to discuss it with Doug. After all, he was always on about God's creation and our responsibility. Sparky agreed with me but Sam, as ever, said she didn't think grown-ups understood. I was beginning to feel she was getting obsessed with her personal crusade against pollution.

I'd almost forgotten. The next day was the youth club outing. A whole day out in the country, away from the city grime, away from home and arguments about the state of my room.

Doug was taking us to a nearby country park. Angelica was going to be there as well. I wasn't really keen, but at least the park had opened a 'traditional farm'. That sounded a bit more fun. We met at the club hut at nine-thirty and piled into the church van for the short trip.

As usual, Lump had brought provisions for a six-month jungle trek. He even began eating before the van door was shut. The rest of us settled down to chat.

We fell out of the van at our destination. It used to be a large house with huge grounds, but was now owned by the local council and open to the public. Within minutes I knew I was going to be bored.

'I've seen more action at the Senior Citizens' Christmas Party than here,' I grumbled, tossing an empty crisp packet in the direction of a bin and missing it by a mile. Lump threw some stuff in the same general direction.

Just then, Sam flipped! She went on and on about

pollution and spoiling the countryside. I mean, at least I'd thrown it in the general direction of the bin. It all seemed over the top to me. There was loads of rubbish lying around the bin so I couldn't be sure which was mine. I pointed this out to Sam. That wasn't a good idea. Doug intervened.

'We have to remember that God created this world for us to *use*, not mess up,' he said. 'It was a beautiful place to start with but people have spent most of their time messing it up.'

Trust him to make me feel guilty. To make it worse, he set about picking up the rubbish himself. I was shamed into helping. Looking round the park though, you could see he was right. God had used some people to build a beautiful place, and now others were coming along and making a right mess of it.

We walked up the drive together in the sunshine. For once, Doug seemed more like his usual cheerful self. Perhaps because we were meeting Angelica at the farm. Sam judged that this might be a good time to talk to him.

'Er, Doug,' she began, 'you know, I think you are *so* right about all this creation stuff.'

'Yes,' said Doug suspiciously.

'Well,' Sam continued, 'don't you think we have a point about that factory then?'

Doug had obviously been expecting this.

He sighed. 'Angelica has had a word with me,' he said in a resigned way. 'You do have a point. But do you have proof? Anyway, you are making your point in the wrong way, Sam. You're usually the one who stops Nick going over the top. Now it seems to be working the other way round.'

I smiled, feeling good.

'Trouble is,' Doug continued, 'Nick isn't very good at that sort of thing.'

I slumped like a punctured balloon.

'Come on,' said Doug, 'let's enjoy ourselves here, and talk about it in the club hut tomorrow evening, OK?'

We had reached the farm. I nudged Sam. I could see she was trying hard not to get all steamed up. She smiled weakly at me, and I felt really relieved. I didn't like all this conflict.

At the entrance we bought some nuts and bread to feed the animals. Lump had to be instructed that they were not for him to eat!

Mo went straight to the old carthorse and reached up to feed him. The rest of us leaned against a low wall to watch. Suddenly there was an almighty 'oink', and a huge pig leapt up in the sty over the wall behind us. We all jumped away, laughing. Well, all but one.

Lump had a different centre of gravity to the rest of us. He fell back into the pigpen, landed in all the muck, and was then chased around the pen by two very noisy pigs. Lump was screaming. The pigs were screaming. We were helpless with laughter. He dived over the gate, reaching a height I had never seen him reach before, and landed with a heavy thud in the yard. Fortunately he was well padded, and didn't really hurt himself. But he was really upset, mainly because he had lost most of his provisions which the pigs were now enjoying.

We tried to clean him up, but he still ponged a lot!

'Where's Angelica?' Sam asked. 'I thought we were meeting her here?'

'We are,' Doug replied. 'Follow me.'

Further into the farm were a row of workshops, which had sounds of activity coming from inside. We followed Doug to investigate. In the first one was Eric with Walter. In the second was Angelica. It was Craft Week on the farm. Angelica was demonstrating furniture making; Eric was carving wood.

We went inside and Doug gave Angelica a peck on the cheek, which brought a loud 'Whoop' from the rest of us. He went bright red and Angelica laughed. Sam suggested we carried on looking round the farm for a while.

'Why?' I demanded.

She just looked at me. Then she nudged me and looked at Doug, who appeared to be very interested in one of Angelica's pieces of furniture. I realized, and giggled. We all moved off, leaving them together.

Eric was very busy setting out his sculptures and wasn't free to talk. So we carried on looking round the farm. We all kept clear of Lump, and he got some very odd looks from the other visitors.

At the Victorian farmhouse, the lady in charge wouldn't let Lump in. That really upset him because she had just made some bread, and was giving out great chunks of it, covered in home-made jam. As a consolation, Chip took some out to poor old Lump. That was not a good idea!

Behind the wall where Lump sat was a beehive. The

jam was very attractive to the bees, who naturally came to investigate. Of course, Lump was not keen on their curiosity. He was not going to give up his bread and jam to anybody, let alone bees. He leapt off the wall and ran away, clutching his trophy with the bees in full chase. He passed Angelica, Doug and Eric at speed. Although the bees soon gave up the chase, Lump didn't stop to check. He hurtled in the direction of the pond near the entrance and dived in!

It wasn't very deep, and he was already dirty, so he didn't care. He sat in the pond, having made sure that his bread and jam stayed dry, beaming in triumph. But just as he was about to take a bite, a goose swam by and plucked it from his hand. He was not amused!

We cleaned off Lump, and after we had finished laughing we walked back to the workshops. Doug was in deep conversation with Eric on one side and Angelica on the other. Then I understood! I could tell from the look on Sam's face. I realized that she and Angelica had been setting this up the other day when I interrupted them.

'Let's go and get ice-creams,' said Sam quickly, marching us all away from the workshop.

Poor Doug couldn't have stood a chance. He didn't say much as he drove us home, but had a big frown on his face. I didnt ask what he was thinking about. He would tell us in his own good time. After all, that was what my chat with God had been about—waiting and being patient. God could sort it out, but I had to trust him.

11
Fire!

The country park had reminded me how much I liked being in the fresh air, so on the way back I suggested that we all go for a bike ride the next day. But I could only get Sparky, Raj and Sam to come. The others all thought of an excuse. Anyone would think I was always getting them into trouble!

I think Sam was happy to come along because both Angelica and Eric would be at the Craft Week at the country park. That meant she couldn't spend yet more time talking with them about all that environmental stuff. That was great!

We cycled off and had a great day hurtling along country lanes with the wind whistling through our hair. When we got to a farm track that we knew, we had races, and then called in at a village shop to buy something to eat and drink, and finally made our way home, cycling along the canal path back to the city.

Along the canalside, we looked for evidence of pollution, and saw plenty. The canal looked really dirty. There were some dead fish and the plants along the canal bank didn't look healthy. It got worse the nearer we got to the city.

Suddenly Raj, who was at the front, slammed on his brakes. We all nearly ploughed into the back of him.

'What are you playing at?' I demanded.

'Look,' he said, 'Look at that.'

We followed his pointing finger to a load of smoke rising from further up the canal.

'Great,' said Sam, 'it looks like the factory is burning down!'

Then we looked at each other.

'Oh no,' Sam and I groaned together.

We grabbed our bikes and cycled furiously in the direction of the smoke. We had to leave the canal, turning up Canal Street, because of the barriers put up by the factory. Further along, we turned down to the canal again. We dropped our bikes at Eric's gate, clambered over, and ran in the direction of the boat. As we rushed down the path, we could see Eric's boat burning. Eric himself was heaving pails of water from the canal and throwing them helplessly on to the fire.

'Raj, go and call a fire engine,' I shouted.

He ran off without arguing. Sam, Sparky and I grabbed what we could to scoop water out of the canal and throw it on the fire.

Suddenly Eric stopped.

'Where's Walter?' he yelled.

'Oh no,' he shouted, 'he's trapped at the front of the boat.'

The fire had taken hold of the middle area and smoke was spreading rapidly to the two ends. I leapt onto the front of the boat with Sparky, and we pulled at the doors, which were locked and bolted.

'Come off, it's not safe,' Eric yelled.

I wasn't giving up that easily. I leapt off the boat and found an old iron rod. Jumping back, I jammed it in the padlock and Sparky and I broke it off. Then we smashed at the doors with our feet and the rod. They gave way and swung open.

Suddenly we were surrounded with smoke from the cabin. Sparky had to turn away, with smoke in his eyes and lungs.

I ducked down and called, 'Walter, Walter.'

I heard a squawk, and up popped a rather bedraggled duck. Not waiting to see if he would peck me, I grabbed him and leapt with Sparky back to the bank. At that moment the fire brigade arrived and set about putting the fire out. I didn't fancy giving Walter the kiss of life, and was mightily relieved he didn't need it. He was very grateful, and quacked his appreciation.

There was nothing else for us to do but watch the fire fighters bringing it under control. A lot of damage had been done to the central area of the boat, but it didn't sink.

By then the police had arrived. A police officer, together with a fireman, began asking questions.

'How did it start?' they asked.

'I don't know,' Eric replied. 'I came back early from my work and left my duck in the boat while I did a little shopping. When I got back it was already burning, and Walter was trapped inside.'

They looked curiously at the duck who quacked in agreement at Eric's story.

'If only ducks could talk,' the policeman muttered.

Once the fire was out, the firemen began poking around to find the cause.

'It appears to be a cooker fire at first look,' one fireman said, 'But it's very difficult to tell with so much wood and other stuff packed in such a small area.'

The police officer went off, with the fireman, making loads of notes in a little book.

We were convinced it was no accident. Maybe we were jumping to conclusions, but there were too many coincidences. It had to be something to do with Hargreaves and his friend, and the factory across the canal.

'Do you think it was an accident, Eric?' Sam asked.

'I don't know,' he replied. 'I am a bit careless, and I do sometimes leave things lying around by the cooker.'

'But isn't it too much of a coincidence, with all that trouble you've had from Hargreaves, the security guard from the factory?'

'Maybe you're right,' Eric replied. 'It is a bit strange that it happened just now. I just don't know.' He was obviously in a bit of a state of shock, so we didn't push it.

The fire fighters started packing up, and the policeman came over to Eric again.

'Right,' the policeman said. 'It appears that the most likely cause was the cooker.'

'That's not right,' Sam butted in. 'I was in there the other day, and it was perfectly safe.'

'Young lady,' the policeman responded huffily, 'those fire fighters are experts at their job, and that is the conclusion they have come to.'

'OK, so it started there, but how?' I butted in. He turned to me. His eyes narrowed as he recognized me.

'You're Sergeant Carter's son, aren't you?' he asked accusingly.

'Yes,' I responded defensively.

'I thought so,' he replied. 'We know all about you and your imagination. Your father has my sympathy!'

I could feel myself getting angry!

Luckily, before I could respond, Raj arrived with Doug.

'I'm terribly sorry,' he said as he came up to Eric. 'What a terrible thing to happen. You must stay with me until it's all sorted out.'

Eric was still a bit dazed by it all and didn't answer.

'Doug,' I butted in, 'the police think a cooker caused it. But we know somebody did it on purpose. It was arson!'

'Just a minute, young man,' the policeman said. 'You, more than anybody, should know not to go around saying things without any evidence. That could get you into very serious trouble. Now, before anything else, I must have statements from you all.'

He took us on one side, one at a time, and took

statements about what had happened at the fire. It was very frustrating—he wasn't interested in what he called our 'wild accusations'.

Doug comforted Eric, who gradually sorted himself out. Doug also tried to calm us down. Eric wouldn't go to Doug's. He had rescued an old tent from the boat to sleep in. 'Then I can look after what's left of my boat,' he insisted.

The policeman left and we helped sort out Eric's things so that he could be reasonably comfortable. Doug was going to come back later with some food, and we all said that we would be around in the morning to help clear up.

As we walked away from the boat, Doug listened to our views on what had happened. I was convinced he would be against our ideas, but I was wrong. He was beginning to understand what was going on. Angelica was obviously getting through to him. He stopped by the gate and explained what he thought about everything.

'You two must be careful not to accuse without definite proof,' he said. 'I have been thinking a lot about what has been happening. It reminds me of something I read in my Bible a couple of days ago.'

I could feel a sermon coming on!

'It was about a character called Jeremiah,' Doug went on. 'It says in Jeremiah, "I, the Lord, command you to do what is right and just. Protect the person who is being cheated from the one who is cheating him".'

'What we must do,' Doug continued, 'is to make

sure first of all, that we ourselves are doing what is right and proper, and then we must protect the person who is being cheated. So I think that we must help Eric, but we must do it in a right and proper way.'

When I first got involved in church and all that Christian stuff, I was a bit worried because I thought it was just for wimps. But it hasn't been like that. It does makes sense, and you certainly can't be a softy. Trouble is, it's not always easy!

I was very keen to hear about sorting out things, and helping Eric—that sounded like a bit of adventure. I wasn't so keen on the 'being right and proper' bit.

Sam didn't say a word. She just looked at her feet.

'So,' Doug went on, 'while we are thinking about the right way to deal with this we have to do the right and proper things in our own lives.'

'What does that mean?' I demanded.

'It means,' Doug said sternly, 'that we go on home for now. It means we apologize to Mr Brown. It means, Nick, that you make sure that you keep your room tidy.'

What a daft thing to say! What had my room got to do with things? My room was my affair. Sorting that factory out was different. I couldn't see any connection. What was needed was action, and fast!

'Oh come on, Doug,' I responded. 'What we ought to be doing is getting round to that factory and sorting that big gorilla Hargreaves out and all the people who pull his strings!'

'On what evidence?' Doug responded sharply.

'Well, let's get some,' Sam butted in.

'All in good time,' Doug replied. 'But the first thing to do is help Eric get his boat back in order.'

'Grown-ups!' I grumbled, got on my bike and rode off. Sam, Sparky and Raj followed. We were four very angry cyclists. We *would* help Eric, but if it was evidence Doug wanted, we would get that too!

12
Scrapers and Sandpaper

I got up very early the next morning and set off to get
the gang together. Mo came along too—everybody
would be needed to help Eric clear up. It was easier
getting some out of bed than others. It was OK calling
for Sam and Sparky next door. Chip was always up
bright and early—but Whizzer. The only time that
Whizzer didn't whizz was first thing in the morning!
And Lump couldn't focus until he had eaten a big
breakfast. So we waited for him. Raj had been ready for
hours. Eventually I had the whole troop ready. This
included my dog Wally, as Mum insisted that he come
along.

I felt a bit like the Pied Piper as I made my way
along Canal Street, explaining what had happened and
how we were going to help Eric get things straight.
When we arrived at the boat, Eric had already got
started. Angelica had brought some wood over, and
Eric was busy knocking out the burnt and damaged
stuff. The boat wasn't too badly damaged and Eric
thought he might be able to mend it himself. But lots

of his things had been burnt.

Walter greeted me with a very friendly quack. I had obviously made a friend for life. I was a bit worried about how Wally and Walter would get on, but I needn't have been. As far as Walter was concerned, any friend of mine was a friend of his, and after some suspicious and very careful sniffing on Wally's part, and further quacking and feather rustling from Walter, they became firm friends, and chased off down the path, woofing and quacking.

Eric put his tools down and jumped onto the bank. 'Thanks for coming,' he said.

We stood around, working out how best we could help. At first he said that he would be all right on his own, but that was just a front and he very quickly gave in to our offers of support. We would have been discussing what to do for ages, but fortunately Angelica and Doug arrived.

Angelica soon sorted Eric out, and started getting things organized. While she and Eric worked on replacing the woodwork, Doug organized the rest of us to strip down the less damaged areas where the paintwork had been blistered by the heat, ready for repainting. Doug sorted us out with scrapers and sandpaper. It was going to be a long and dirty job, just the sort I liked. Fortunately, everyone was in old clothes and got stuck in. Even Lump joined in, especially when Eric sent Whizzer and Raj to the shops to get cans of drink and biscuits. We worked very hard till lunch, cracking jokes and singing to keep us going.

Eric had stopped early to cook up an amazing bowl of stuff on his camp fire. I was a bit suspicious of all the funny beans and mush he was throwing in, but all the work had made me hungry. It was actually very tasty, and I had seconds, much to Sam's amusement.

'All that fuss you've made in the past about vegetarian food,' she laughed, 'You don't seem to be objecting now!'

'This is great,' I responded, 'but I can't do without some flesh to chew on!'

It had the effect I thought it would.

'Yuck, you are vile,' she complained.

I laughed and she threw a hunk of bread at me.

After lunch we were able to start repainting in places. Sparky, Sam and Mo worked on the back of the boat while the rest of us concentrated on the front end.

'It's called the bow,' Doug explained.

'Aye, aye, captain,' I replied. He threw a cloth at me and I nearly overbalanced into the canal. That should have warned us to be careful!

Raj and I worked on the outside, painting the side of the boat facing the towpath. Eric was going to turn the boat round later for us to work on the other side.

At the stern, Sparky was doing the same. Mo and Chip worked inside the boat; Sam, Lump and Whizzer on the bow and stern and on top.

It was a nice day, and we were doing something good for Eric, and that made me feel good. Doug was moving around and helping different people, but I noticed he was being particularly helpful to Angelica, who needed less help than anybody.

I had completely lost Wally and Walter, but I could hear a lot of barking and quacking coming from the bushes down the towpath. Wally was a very strange dog, but Walter was an extremely weird duck, and anyway behaved more like a dog! Eric told us he had owned a lovely old dog, which had found this tiny baby duckling one day and brought it back in her mouth to Eric. Between them they nursed it back to health. Walter was devoted to the dog right until the day she died. But before she died, the dog had taught Walter to be a good watch dog, and now the confused duck didn't know whether it was a dog or a duck!

Just at that moment both Walter and Wally were behaving like silly puppies. They were playing something like hide and seek, followed by a wild chase. Every so often they leapt out of the undergrowth and chased up and down the towpath. I turned back to my job, not noticing that they were getting nearer and nearer to the boat with their game. Suddenly they came charging out past Eric's tent and hurtled along the path right by the boat.

Sparky's can of paint went flying, and then Sparky himself was knocked over, landing in the spilt paint. Then Wally and Walter raced back into the under-growth.

I roared with laughter. Sparky roared with anger as he wiped paint from his clothes. Then the terrible two came hurtling out of the bushes again, right behind me. I was still laughing at Sparky when suddenly I was mixed up in a whirlwind of hair and feathers, barks and quacks. Wally did try to avoid me. He changed direction with his little legs, but the trouble was his fat body carried on, pushed by a crazy duck.

I could feel myself falling, and grabbed at the boat, forgetting the wet paint. My hands slipped and slid along the boat, ruining all my work. I had to keep grabbing furiously until I just managed to regain my balance. And no, I didn't fall in!

Raj, who was working alongside me, took a different escape route. He saw the beasts coming and leapt up on to the boat. Unfortunately he leapt straight onto where Doug was standing. Doug, of course, was gazing along the boat to where Angelica was working, in a world of his own. They collided, and both slipped in the wet paint. Raj slid gracefully across the boat, and off the other side, landing in the canal. Doug cannoned off sideways into the well of the boat where Lump was working.

'Whoa!' yelled Raj, followed by a huge splash.

'Whoa!' yelled Doug, followed by another 'Whoa!' from Lump as Doug descended on top of him. This was followed by 'Owwwww,' as Doug made contact, landing on Lump and rolling off into more wet paint. So Lump jumped up on to the top of the boat, where he made contact with the wet paint splashed by Doug and Raj. He slipped, he slid. An Olympic iceskater couldn't have done better. He moved gracefully across the boat, over the edge, kersplash into the water.

The animals rushed off into the safety of the bushes as I tried to heave the helpless Lump from the water. Everybody else was paralyzed with laughter! My hands were slippery from the paint, and he just kept falling back, with even bigger splashes, and yet louder howls of agony.

Eventually the others got control of themselves and came along to help. Getting Raj out was easy, but it took the combined work of Sparky, Eric, Angelica and myself to heave the unfortunate Lump out. Doug took them both home, remembering how sick I had been after falling in the canal.

Wally and Walter made themselves scarce for ages, hoping that we would forget what they had done. But we forgave them very easily, because by the end of the day, and in spite of the setback and spilt paint, there had been a tremendous amount of work done.

Eric was very grateful. When Doug got back we sat and had a cup of tea and loads of cake admiring our work. Narrow boats were very beautiful, especially if you had painted them yourself.

'I should be able to finish the undercoat tomorrow,' Eric said. 'There is just some primer needed on the bits that Angelica and I have rebuilt. Finishing off the inside will be easy too.'

'That should show the great gorilla from the factory we are not easily beaten,' I said.

'Yeah. I still think we should do something about that factory,' said Sam, looking round at everybody, but trying not to catch Doug's warning glance.

'Something has to be done,' Eric replied, 'but I'm not sure it's something for you to do.'

'Why not?' I added aggressively.

'For a start, I don't want a lot of fuss yet.' Eric went on, 'What I need is to build up evidence. Why do you think they are so keen to move me on? I've been recording all the things I've seen. It was unfortunate that one day when I was out they stole my camera and film, and that has slowed me down. They are also trying to move me on by threatening me. I happen know that they are trying to buy the land on this side of the canal and build another factory, completely closing the area off.'

'Did you know this?' I asked Doug.

'I found out from Angelica and Eric what was going on when I visited the farm,' he replied.

'The trouble is,' added Angelica, 'that we have hardly any *real* proof about all this so far. That's why we don't want you all to get too involved.'

Eric nodded, as did Doug. An adult conspiracy!! We just looked at each other and said nothing. I decided it was time to keep quiet.

'Come on, gang,' I said. 'It's time to go.'

I finally retrieved Wally, who came up to me with his soppiest look trying to avoid a telling-off. My mind was on other things—lucky for Wally.

That night, Lump was very ill. He was so sick he had to be taken to hospital. Although Lump ate such an awful load of rubbish, the world's greatest human dustbin, we knew it must have been the water he took in as he kept falling in the canal. Raj had been very careful not to swallow any water and was OK.

We knew what had made Lump so ill, and that made us even more determined to sort that factory out. But how?

13
Collecting the Evidence

'What *are* we going to do about it then?' I asked Sparky and Sam as we sat in the club hut next day, downing cans of coke.

'About what?' Sparky responded numbly.

'Has somebody switched your light out or is it just that your battery's run down?' I said impatiently. 'About the factory. About Eric, Lump and all the other things that have happened.'

It all went quiet as we struggled to think of something. I could see the tortured look on Sam's face, and Sparky's blank stare. I tried to kick my brain cells into action.

'I've got an idea,' Sam suddenly said. 'What about going to see Miss Fox?'

'Great,' I replied, 'I'm all for it, but why?' Miss Fox was a brilliant teacher, and I don't say that about many. She had all the boys eating out of her hand. She was so good-looking. She only had to look at me and my knees went all wobbly. The girls thought she was great because she was so clever, much brighter than the other teachers. Too good to be true really!

'I know that you're so stuck on her that you don't even know what subject she takes you for,' Sam complained, 'but she does happen to be our science teacher, and she has spent most of the last term talking about the environment.'

'Has she?' I asked innocently.

Sam glared at me.

'Anyway, why should we go and see her?' I continued.

'Well,' Sam said, 'we could go down to the canal and get some water samples. And then we could ask her to test them for us.'

Great idea! Why didn't we think of it before? Why didn't I think of it? Action at last! Sam went off to find out where Miss Fox lived. Sparky and I went home looking for jars with lids and some string. The string was easy. I had miles of it in one of my collections. But the jars—we devised a plan for removing them without having to tell our mums what we were up to. That would only complicate matters.

Sparky's mum was easy. While I distracted her in the garden, talking about nothing in particular, Sparky ferreted about in the kitchen and picked up two jars. He put them behind the front wall, and then we went for the difficult one.

My mum!

After we'd collected the string from my bedroom, Sparky got talking to Mum in the hall, and it worked for a while.

I crept into the kitchen. Unfortunately, Wally

decided to help! As I nosed around looking for jars, Wally nosed around. He didn't know what he was looking for, but he was determined to be helpful. The trouble was that although Wally's nose was attached to the rest of his body, the rest of his body was bigger, fatter and out of control.

We were digging around in a cupboard, and I was trying to push the stupid dog out of the way as quietly as possible, which he thought was part of a great game. As his nose dug around in the cupboard, with me pushing him away, his tail began to show his excitement. It started to wag furiously. It wagged so much it was moving the rest of him from side to side. First he knocked over packets, but suddenly one enormous wag caught some empty milk bottles and they went crashing across the floor.

'What's going on in there?' Mum asked suspiciously from the hall where she was talking to Sparky.

'Wuff,' I responded.

Mum wasn't fooled.

'Nick, what are you up to?' she demanded.

I stood up, banging my head on the cupboard shelf, as Mum walked in followed by an apologetic-looking Sparky.

'I was just looking for something,' I said lamely as I rubbed my head.

'What?' Mum asked, narrowing her eyes.

'Oh, just a couple of old jars,' I went on.

'What for?' the inquisition continued.

It was worse than being in court. Now, I wasn't going to lie. The next answer was crucial. 'To do some science,' I replied, honestly and innocently. It worked.

'OK,' she said. 'It just so happens that I've got some I was about to throw out.'

She handed them over and we escaped quickly before there were any more questions. After putting all the jars together in a carrier bag, we sat on the wall to wait for Sam. We didn't have to wait long.

'Do you want the good news or the bad news?' she started.

'Go on,' I said.

'The good news is that I've found out where Miss Fox lives,' she went on. 'The bad news is that she lives in a flat at Mrs Davies' house.'

'Not Dragon Davies, the mad musician,' I groaned, thinking of our fearsome music teacher.

'The very same,' Sam confirmed.

We all sat on the wall, head in hands, sunk in gloom.

'Come on,' I said at last. 'We'll think of a way round that when we get to it. Let's get the first bit done first.'

The others agreed and we picked up the jars and set off.

On the way we called in at Lump's house to see how he was, and we were very pleased to hear that he was making a quick recovery. He had just had his first fix of chips and pizza, and was feeling much better. Nothing kept him away from food for long.

We also called in on Angelica but she was out. Finally we reached Eric, who was putting the final touches to his repaired boat.

Walter was disappointed to find that Wally was not with us, but he was still happy to see me, his hero, and gave a welcoming quack.

We told Eric what we were going to do, and he thought it was a great idea. He couldn't see how we could get into bother doing it. He even suggested some good places to take samples, and told us how to do the job properly.

Walter came along, but Eric went back to his beloved narrow boat. The duck watched us fasten string round the tops of jars and toss them into the canal at different points. After pulling them out we sealed them with the lids. Now we had four pieces of evidence.

We labelled the jars and did a simple map to show where we had taken the samples, then set off carrying them carefully, in the direction of the dragon's lair! It was quite a way, and the jars were heavy, filled with vile-looking and smelly liquid.

The house we were looking for was up a tree-lined avenue, set back from the road. It looked like Dracula's Castle to me, but Sam said I was imagining things. I wasn't imagining the dreaded Dragon Davies!

We rang the bell and waited. A dark shadow grew on the other side of the glass. The outline was unmistakable. I could almost see the horns! The door opened. Without thinking, we all took a step back in fright. Dragon Davies towered above us, glaring down. Her eyes narrowed when she saw me.

'What do you want?' she demanded.

'Is Miss Fox in, please?' Sam asked politely.

'Why do you want to see her?' growled the Dragon.

'Er, we want some help with some science,'

Sparky said, struggling for words.

'What are those disgusting things?' went on Dragon, pointing at the dirty jam jars.

'They are samples for Miss Fox to test,' I said earnestly.

'Samples of what?' she asked, screwing up her face in disgust.

I was tempted to tell her something horrible, but Sam said, 'It's canal water.'

The Dragon drew herself up to her full height and said, 'Well, take them away. Miss Fox is not due back until tomorrow, and I'm not having those dreadful things in the house. And besides,' she went on, 'you shouldn't be bothering her in the holidays. Go away.'

She slammed the door in our faces. Well, she shut it actually.

We stood there in silence. Without saying a word, all three of us at the same time, stuck out our tongues.

'I saw that,' came a voice to our left. It was Dragon Davies, looking through her window.

We turned and ran, struggling not to break the jars. We didn't stop until we reached the end of the street.

'What do we do now?' I demanded. 'We can't keep on carrying these things about.'

'Let's put them behind that wall over there,' Sparky suggested, 'and try again when Miss Fox is back.' He was pointing to the wall of the local primary school. It was the summer holidays, and no one was there, so they would be safe enough.

'A good idea,' I agreed quickly, and we hid them in a patch of bushes behind the school wall.

Sam wasn't so sure, but we didn't give her time to argue.

We made our way back home, feeling rather let down. It had been a brilliant idea. By then I was desparately thirsty, so we dropped in at the club hut.

Comfortably settled in the old chairs, with cool cans of Coke in our sweaty hands, we recovered from our ordeal. Doug appeared as we sat talking about it, and so we told him our story. I think I rather overdid the Dracula's Castle bit.

After I had finished, Doug said quietly that he wanted to have a word with me. I didn't like the sound of that. Sam and Sparky went off home rather quickly, and we settled down in the chairs.

'How is Angelica?' I teased Doug, 'When are you going to propose?'

It threw him off his stride and he blushed furiously, so I knew it was serious. It probably wasn't the right thing to say just then.

'Nick,' he said, recovering himself and changing the subject, 'your mum has been talking to me. She's more than a bit cross at the way you have been behaving. It comes back to the same old thing about saying all those things about behaving in a Christian way outside the home, and then doing the opposite when you're with your family.'

My joking mood changed suddenly. I felt like a punctured balloon. It hurt, because I thought I was so much better than I used to be.

'Don't get me wrong,' Doug went on. 'You're a different lad from the one I used to know. But becoming a Christian doesn't mean it's all automatic. You have to keep working at things, especially with those close to you.'

I mumbled something to Doug about having to go, and sloped off. I was fed up with grown-ups always wanting more. I was fed up with myself. I didn't know what to do with the feelings and angry thoughts going round in my head. All because my room was in a mess, and I wouldn't help around the house and stuff like that. I knew Doug was right and that made it worse.

I kicked a stone angrily against the kerb. It felt good so I kicked it harder. This time it hit the top of the kerb, flew high up into the air, and over the nearby fence.

My heart sank before I heard the crash. I knew where Mr Grant's greenhouse was. I knew that, with the whole garden to fall in, that stone would be magnetically drawn to the greenhouse.

I groaned. Why did it always happen to me?

14
Blushes for Nick

I didn't run away. I knew I had to go and own up to Mr Grant. He was quite a kindly man, I'd known him all my life. Anyway, it wasn't his fault that I was a bit cross. So I went and explained what I'd done. He was angry to begin with, but I have discovered that getting in an apology early takes the steam out of things.

I negotiated a deal with him which meant paying him my next three weeks' pocket money. It hurt, but at least it stopped him going to my dad! I turned away from Mr Grant's front gate and shrugged my shoulders as I set off for home. Then I noticed Doug walking towards me.

'What's up?' he demanded.

That made me feel even worse, but I told him.

'That was a stupid thing to do,' Doug commented.

'What, paying out my pocket money to repair the glass?' I asked.

'No, you fool,' he said, 'breaking the window in the first place. What you did after that was dead right, and very impressive.'

That made me feel better, a little, but three weeks without pocket money was going to hurt. Still, I felt that Doug and I were back on good terms, which was something.

I went home and had some tea, then wandered out to the wall outside my house. Sitting there was a favourite hobby of mine. That wall was like an old friend. I even talked to it—something I wouldn't admit to anyone! Sam and Sparky came out and joined me. I told them about the broken glass. They didn't laugh, they knew what three weeks' lost pocket money felt like. We sat there, kicking our heels in silence.

'How are we going to get the samples to Miss Fox?' Sparky asked. Our brains were working very slowly. I'd had beans on toast for tea—always affects my brain.

'I've got an idea,' I said, suddenly bursting into life. 'We could wait by the school opposite the road her flat is in. Then, when she comes along we can give her the jars.'

'That's stupid,' Sam replied. 'We can't sit there all day until she comes.'

'Have you got a better idea?' I demanded sharply.

'Well no, not at the moment,' she admitted, 'but I will,' and left in a bit of a huff.

'Right, Sparky,' I said. 'Let's get things sorted out. I can't wait for one of Sam's bright ideas, we've got to get on.'

Sparky and I organized a simple rota so that either he or I would be there all through the day. Sparky took the first shift, getting Raj to help him. I took over around lunchtime. Sam refused to be a part of it; Lump was still a bit under the weather; Whizzer wouldn't get up; Mo was busy; so I was left with Chip! He didn't want to come, but I 'persuaded' him!

'Why don't we just go to the house?' Chip asked innocently as we waited at the school wall with the jam jars.

When I reminded him whose house it was he visibly shook. The terror on his face at the thought of Dragon Davies brought back memories of the time at school when Chip attempted to repair the piano after he dropped his chewing gum into it, just as the Dragon came into the room. It was funny to everyone except Chip and Dragon Davies!

Time passed slowly and it was very boring. I practised what I would say to Miss Fox. The first thing would be to carry her bags for her. I would do that. Chip could carry the jars. I hoped my knees wouldn't collapse when I tried to talk to her. Just the thought of it gave me butterflies in my stomach!

'Have you got a crush on Miss Fox?' Chip asked innocently when I outlined the plan. I pushed him over the wall!

The road was very quiet, and hardly a car passed by. We could see in both directions and up the avenue to Dragon Davies' house. It hadn't even entered my head that she wouldn't come along the road from the bus stop, so when a taxi drove down the street it didn't make any particular impression. As it stopped to turn into the avenue, there was the beautiful Miss Fox looking out at me. My mouth dropped open. She just looked in surprise and then waved. I waved back with my mouth open. I must have looked a complete nut!

The taxi drove on. After a moment's blankness I woke up, grabbed the jars and hurtled off after it. I got no more than ten yards. In my blankness I hadn't take any account of kerbstones. My toes did. I hit them at full speed. My body carried on, leaving my feet behind until they were forced to follow. At that point I shot like a rocket through a small hedge. The jars were left behind. I arrived about two centimetres from a pair of garden shears held by a rather startled old man. His pet poodle licked my nose.

'Good afternoon,' I said politely, 'Nice day.'

I picked myself up, dusted myself down, and walked out of the gate back onto the pavement. There I saw some very broken jars and then I turned and saw the taxi disappearing up the drive to the Dragon's lair. I turned to see Chip's legs wriggling in the air. He had fallen backwards over the wall in uncontrollable laughter.

I knew there was no point in telling him not to repeat what he had seen, I would just have to face the gang. What was worse was having to face Sam and tell her about the jars.

Chip and I made our way home, slowly.

Sam was waiting for me. When I told her, I expected that she would be cross about the jars. She actually had great difficulty staying on our front wall, she was laughing so much.

'Miss Fox said that she had seen you,' Sam said

when she had stopped laughing.

'What do you mean?' I asked.

'Well,' she went on, 'when I rang her to ask her advice about what to do, she said that she had seen you sitting on the school wall, waving and grinning like one of those laughing clowns you see at the fun-fair.'

My heart hit the soles of my feet, and I blushed. Not a delicate pink, but a deep beetroot red. Sam had no sympathy!

'Well, actually, she didn't use those exact words,' said Sam, softening. 'But you really are a complete unthinking idiot at times, Nick,' she said. 'And I ought never to speak to you again. I can't think how I put up with you.'

I looked, and felt, pathetic.

'Miss Fox has offered to help us if we write it up as a project next term,' Sam continued. I groaned! Miss Fox was just like all the rest.

'She hasn't got the equipment to test the samples herself,' Sam went on, 'but she knows someone who has. We've got to get some fresh samples tomorrow and meet her outside the club hut.'

I nodded weakly in agreement. What else could I do?

We wandered over to the club and met Doug. When we told him about Miss Fox he thought we had done the right thing—after a bit of persuasion. We decided to go and tell Eric. The rest of the gang were about, so we all went down to the canal together.

When we got to Eric's boat we were surprised to see everything packed up. He was about to leave.

'What's happening?' demanded Sam.

'I've decided to take my boat down the canal to safety,' he replied. 'I don't want it getting damaged again, and I don't want anyone getting hurt on my account, so I thought it was for the best. I'm heading for the Basin.'

'I hope you're not doing this just for us,' I said. 'Because we can stick up for ourselves.'

Eric turned to me. 'Look, Nick,' he said, 'I don't like violence of any kind. I haven't given up the fight, I am just choosing to carry on my argument another way.'

It sounded like running to me, but I didn't say anything! He offered us a ride on the boat just as far as the lock, and we all accepted.

We were a pretty quiet bunch of people as the boat made its way down the canal. It didn't help to see Mr Brown and his henchmen from the factory smirking as we went past. It didn't help to pass through the dead fish and all the other results of pollution.

It would be a lot harder for Eric working from the Basin. It was a long way out of the city, and a long way to the craft shop where he sold most of his beloved sculptures. But at least he could start to earn some money repairing boats.

At the lock we hopped off and helped him get his boat through. There was a sad croak from a quiet Walter, and a forlorn wave from Eric as he carried on down the canal. We turned for the walk back.

'I am *not* going to let that factory win,' muttered Sam.

I put my arm round her. She didn't object. We all felt gutted.

The next afternoon Doug tried to cheer us up by suggesting a game of pitch-and-putt golf in the local park. Nobody was enthusiastic.

'Come on,' he said. 'It's not all over. We're going to collect all the evidence and then we'll WHOP that lot out of sight.'

We were all a bit startled by the WHOP, but it had the desired effect.

'Yeah,' I added, 'when have we ever been beaten before? Come on, you lot. Back into the attack tomorrow. As for now, let's take it out on a few golf balls.'

We hired out a couple of clubs each and set off round the small nine-hole golf course. Lump, Mo, Chip and Whizzer set off in front where we could keep an eye on them. It would slow the rest of us down, but was safer. I mean, they didn't have the control and sophistication of Sparky and Sam and me.

I reckoned it was better to be well behind Lump anyway. He didn't look at all safe with one of those clubs in his hands. It was all right to begin with, and we got halfway round safely. Very big scores, but safely.

The fifth hole was quite a long one, and the first group were ready to start as the rest of us reached the fourth green just behind. Only Doug was in a bunker, the rest were on the green. Those of us in the second group stopped to watch the others tee off. Whizzer hit his into the distance. Then Mo sent a soft one off not very far. Chip took a great deal of time with hundreds of practice swings, and then with great skill, hit the ball about ten metres. The rest of us fell about laughing.

Then it was Lump's turn. He was determined not to get laughed at like Chip so he set about preparing to hit the ball halfway back to the youth club. He took an enormous swing, and the club came down with a mighty swish. The trouble is, when you try to hit it hard, you tend to lose direction. Just to the right of the tee was an enormous oak tree! Lump made a terrific connection with the ball and it shot away, straight at the tree, hitting it at speed. The ball rebounded, returning to Lump at the same speed that it left him. He dived to the ground and the ball passed over him, hit Whizzer on the foot as he fell backwards trying to avoid it.

That took all the speed off the ball, which was just as well, because it hit Chip on the back of the head, fell onto our green and rolled expertly into the fourth hole.

Those who hadn't fallen to the ground taking avoiding action fell to the ground laughing. It was the best hole-in-one I had ever seen.

Lump retrieved the ball and tried again, better this time. It was Doug's turn to get out of the bunker. To begin with he had difficulty because his eyes were watering from laughing so much. Then he had a different sort of difficulty.

He swatted.

'That's five,' I said flatly.

He swished.

'Six,' I added. The ball was still in the bunker.

He thrashed.

'Seven,' I went on, looking at him and trying to keep my face straight.

Doug's face was turning a funny shade of pink. His lips were getting very thin. His smile had gone. He turned away from me and gave the ball an almighty swipe.

The ball soared out of the bunker. It soared over the green. It soared over the trees and over a fence. And then in the distance I heard the most wonderful sound—the crash of breaking glass.

I looked at Doug. The pinkness had turned a very red colour. I looked him in the eye.

'That was a stupid thing to do,' I said with a very straight face. 'I hope you've got plenty of pocket money to spare.'

Doug looked at me. He didn't say a word. Well, what could he say?

15
Meet the Professor

When children break windows it's called being naughty. They get told off and lose all their pocket money. When grown-ups break windows it's called an accident. They have a joke about it and then split the cost. I don't understand this. I'm sure I will when I grow up, but just at the moment it doesn't seem right!

Doug got away with his little tantrum over the golf ball very cheaply, especially when the man who owned the greenhouse saw that he was a vicar!

'OK,' Doug said, reading my mind as we left the park, 'I was a bit silly. You don't have to say anything.'

'Whatever made you think I was going to say anything?' I replied with a big grin on my face. He gave me a funny look. I decided it was best not to tease any more and dropped the subject.

We all went our separate ways. I was going home to watch TV and have an early night. Doug thought I must be sickening for something, but I wasn't. I was just tired, and figured I needed to work on creating a good impression on Mum!

The next morning I was raring to go. Sam, Sparky and I were going to get some fresh canal-water samples. This time Doug and Angelica had supplied us with plastic bottles, given my record for falling over.

We made our way down to the canal, and had a shock. We came to the old gate which used to lead up to Eric's patch and it was all nailed up. Eric hadn't done it, and it didn't take a lot of working out to figure out who had. What a cheek! However, no nailed-up gate was going to stop us.

We went back to Angelica's and borrowed an old box. When Angelica heard what we were up to, she wasn't keen, but I managed to persuade her. She told us to call back in an hour, otherwise she would be coming after us.

The box helped us reach the top of the fence, and the jump down the other side wasn't too bad. Sam tossed the plastic bottles over and then followed. We would have to worry about how to get back over later. I hoped we wouldn't have to do it in a hurry.

'Right, let's split up,' Sam said. 'That way we'll be finished quicker.'

Sam went one way, Sparky went the other. I went to the place where Eric's boat had been moored. It was very sad to see the mooring abandoned. I hoped that we could find a way to get Eric and Walter back. I tossed the jar in and dragged it out. The water really looked mucky. I wasn't very keen to get my hands wet in case I picked any germs up. I looked across at the factory and although a lot of noise was coming from it,

I didn't see anyone looking my way.

That moment, Sam and Sparky came back.

'They've made the fences really big now, with barbed wire on the top and a locked gate at the end,' Sparky said.

'It's the same at the other end,' Sam added. 'That lot over there haven't wasted any time, have they?'

We nodded in agreement.

'OY!' The shout from down the towpath suddenly shook us out of our thoughts. It was Hargreaves, the security guard from the factory. He must have dashed out to the nearest bridge and come up without Sam noticing. He had a bunch of keys in his hand—he must have a key to the locked gate.

'I don't think we should hang around for a chat,' I said to the others. 'Come on, let's scarper.'

We dashed back to the gate. Then I remembered that we hadn't thought of how to get back over. I had hoped for a bit of time to think. Now I was trying to work it out on the run, and there were no answers coming to mind.

We reached the fence and looked at each other. The great hulk of Mr Hargreaves was crashing down the path towards us. What on earth were we going to do? I looked at the others and saw a mixture of panic and fear in their eyes.

Suddenly a face appeared over the fence. 'Need a hand?' Angelica asked brightly.

'Throw the box over,' I demanded, with panic in my voice.

Angelica's head dropped down and the box

appeared. I grabbed it and put it against the fence. I almost threw Sam over—panic makes you really strong!

We passed over the jars quickly and then Sparky leapt over. I followed on his heels just as Hargreaves reached the box. He couldn't get through because the gate was all nailed up. His huge face appeared over the fence, and just as quickly disappeared when his weight proved too much for the box.

'Oyyyouchh!' was the strange shout that came from him. However, he had seen Angelica, and I hoped that wouldn't cause problems for her.

'What was all that about?' she asked.

'Look,' I replied as we walked back to her workshop, 'you'll have to get used to this sort of thing, Angelica. If you're going to spend as much time as you seem to be doing with Doug, that is.'

She blushed. My worst suspicions were confirmed. There was definitely something serious here.

We set off back to the club hut after saying goodbye to Angelica. I warned her to keep clear of the factory. I felt Doug would want me to do that. Back at the hut we settled down to wait for Miss Fox. I went to comb my hair and smarten up. Sam looked at me. 'You don't comb your hair when you come to see me,' she said a touch aggressively.

I blushed! I couldn't think of anything to say that wouldn't incriminate me further. When Miss Fox came along the road, I could feel the butterflies churning in my stomach.

'Hello,' she said brightly.

'Hi,' replied Sam and Sparky. I mumbled something, too tongue-tied to answer.

'Shall we go inside?' Sam said.

We stepped into the club hut. Miss Fox was impressed, particularly when she heard how we had raised the money to build it, and done all the decorating ourselves. Doug arrived and we introduced him.

'I have been thinking about what you said,' Miss Fox said. 'I was at university here, and one of my lecturers would help you out, I am sure. I would do it myself, but I can't get into the labs at school until the start of term.'

'Go on,' added Sam.

'Before I do, you won't forget that you are going to write this up as a project, will you?' said Miss Fox.

I nodded dumbly. In the back of my brain I knew that I didn't like this idea, but I was putty in her hands. Doug smirked, Sam scowled at me.

'Right,' she continued, 'The lecturer I know who could help you lives close by, a Professor Sprottles.'

'Oh, I know the Professor,' Doug butted in. 'Why didn't I think of that?'

'Great,' I added, trying to sound intelligent. 'Let's go and see him.'

Miss Fox and Doug looked at me, then at each other. I 'm sure I saw a twinkle in Doug's eye.

'OK,' he said, 'Why don't I take us all over in the club van?'

In the van I tried to make intelligent conversation with our beautiful science teacher, with Sam and

Sparky behind her sticking their fingers in their throats and pretending to be sick.

We arrived at what looked like an ordinary sort of house.

'The Professor is a bit eccentric,' Miss Fox said on the way, 'but I have rung up and explained the situation.'

I wanted to make a good impression on Miss Fox and so was very eager to ring the bell and do all the talking. The door was opened by a strange-looking woman in old clothes who had white hair tied back in a tight bun. I thought this must be the housekeeper. Professors must have housekeepers. They always did in films! 'I would like to speak to Professor Sprottles,' I demanded in my poshest voice.

'Yes,' came the reply from the strange lady.

'Take me to the Professor,' I insisted in a louder voice, presuming that the old lady was a bit deaf.

'Yes,' came the reply, even louder.

I turned round in exasperation.

'I can't get through to the housekeeper . . .' I said. Then I noticed everybody trying not to laugh.

'Hello, Professor,' Miss Fox said as she brushed past me.

I was mortified.

'Do professors have to be men?' Miss Fox said as she turned back to me.

I shrank to the size of a mouse in my head, and wished I could fall down a hole. Instead, I followed the others into the house, carrying the bottles. I didn't say much during the rest of the visit.

The house was big, piled high with books in every possible space. The furniture was old, but it was clean and tidy. The Professor's husband arrived. He seemed to be the one that kept things in order. He was a doctor at the hospital and suddenly disappeared when a bleeper started sounding in his top pocket.

The Professor and Miss Fox disappeared into a room full of scientific equipment and we sat around and waited. It wasn't long before they came out and sat with us.

'Well?' Sam asked.

'The samples you gave us are very badly polluted,' the Professor said. 'I need to do a lot more tests, but I can tell you straight away that they are very bad.'

'How long will it take?' Doug asked.

'Oh, a few days,' she went on. 'Jane and I will work on it together.'

At last I knew her name. That would be worth a few sweets back at school!

'Thanks for your help,' said Doug. 'I don't know how we will use the information yet, but I am sure it will help our cause.'

It was great to feel that at last Doug was really with us.

'I hope all your efforts will be successful,' Professor Sprottles answered. 'When my husband and I heard what you were doing, we were very keen to help.'

'Well, we'll be going now,' said Doug. 'Thank you. Come on, you lot.'

'I'll stay with the Professor,' Miss Fox said.

When we got back to the hut, Sam wasn't speaking

to me. What had I done now? She walked off, saying she was going home.

'You really are dumb,' Doug said to me. 'When are you going to start thinking before you speak?'

I only half understood what he was talking about. It wasn't my fault the professor was a woman! On the way home Sparky explained—I needed to apologize to Sam. I felt really embarrassed when Sparky started talking about my crush on Miss Fox. It sounded really stupid now. I realized again what an idiot I had looked, and how I might have upset Sam.

When we got home, I stood on the pavement outside Sam's window and called up, 'Sam! Sam!'

She opened the window and glared down.

'I'm sorry, I've been stupid again,' I said.

'Good,' she replied.

'Am I forgiven?' I asked.

She disappeared back into the room and then reappeared, this time with a bucket. The water soaked me to the skin. It was cold and came down with a lot of force, flattening my hair. I spluttered!

'You are now,' she replied.

Sparky leaned out of his window laughing fit to burst. I just stood there looking pathetic!

16
Down at the Basin

It wasn't only Sparky who was watching our touching reconciliation. I turned round and there was Mum, splitting her sides.

'Whatever you did to Sam, I'm sure you deserved it,' she said.

I couldn't argue. I just walked, or should I say dripped, my way into our kitchen and removed most of my clothes for Mum to put them in the washer. Between my mum and Sparky the whole neighbourhood would know about it by the end of the day, so I thought it best to lie low.

That evening I had a phone call from Doug.

'I hope you haven't caught a cold,' he laughed into the phone.

I didn't answer.

The real reason he was ringing was to tell me that Eric had invited us all to visit him at his new mooring in the Basin. Doug was going to take us all down for the day in the van. I knew I would get ribbed, but it sounded like a good day out, so I agreed to go.

The next morning Sam, Sparky, Mo and I were picked up outside our houses. The rest of the gang were already inside. Angelica sat with Doug in the front.

I survived a whole load of comments about water and getting caught in the rain. There was nothing I could do but sit it out until everybody gave up. Once, I used to react to it all, but I discovered that it only made things worse. Of course, we all noticed Doug and Angelica holding hands. This gave me the opportunity to change the subject.

'Er, Doug', I said, 'Shouldn't you be holding the steering wheel with *both* hands?'

'Whe-hey,' everybody shouted.

But instead of blushing, Doug and Angelica laughed. He did put both hands on the wheel, but Angelica was still sitting very close to him.

Eric's new mooring was in a beautiful spot. There were a number of narrow boats there, and lots of interesting buildings, all restored to how they looked when they were first built.

Eric was waiting for us. As soon as Walter saw us he squawked happily and ruffled his feathers. He was even more delighted when he saw Wally had come along as well. They soon disappeared in the tangle of ropes and barges.

'Why don't you all go exploring while I talk to Doug and Angelica?' Eric said. 'I have, er, warned the rest of the people who live here that you would be around.'

'What do you mean?' Sam demanded.

'It's all right', Eric went on. 'I told them what you were trying to do, and they all want you to have a good time.' That sounded better.

All the people who lived on the boats here had little businesses. Some of them had already moved down the canal from Eric's old moorings. They were trying to make the Basin a nice place for people to visit as well as buy the things they made.

Lump's nose soon led him in the direction of one particular building. It was where they were making rock. We all followed Lump's nose. A man and a woman were rolling out a huge lump of stuff on a long table. Then they cut it up into short bits and started wrapping it.

'Do you want to have a go?' the woman asked.

We had to thoroughly wash our hands, and put on all sorts of clothing, including hairnets! When we returned, there was another lump of stuff ready for us. It was warm to the touch, and we all rolled it out and pulled it until it stretched up and down the table. Then we cut it up into bits, put a twist in each bit and wrapped them in see-through paper. We couldn't take them straight away, but had to leave them to get really cool.

'I bet you enjoyed that,' I said to Lump.

He didn't say anything, just nodded. Then I noticed his cheeks were bursting. The greedy thing had been stuffing bits of rock into his mouth until he couldn't get any more in.

Whizzer decided to do something about it. As we went out the door saying our thank yous, Whizzer 'accidentally' trod on Lump's toe. Now Lump never liked to waste food, so it was like a volcano about to erupt. His face went red as he tried to control the pain. But you could see the eruption building up. We all dived for cover. Whizzer didn't make it.

'Whoow!' yelled Lump, grabbing his toe.

'Yeeuch,' went Whizzer as lumps of half-eaten rock sprayed down his neck! As Whizzer went off to clean himself up and Lump went to look for more food, the rest of us set off to explore.

We heard the sound of fairground music, coming from a big shed. We were amazed at what we saw behind the big green doors—a fully working round-about, filled with bobbing horses. It was huge and beautiful, with lights highlighting the colours of the horses and old-fashioned fairground music coming from the middle.

The roundabout slowed to a stop and a heavily-whiskered old man appeared.

'Like it?' he asked.

'It's wonderful,' Mo said for all of us.

'Are you the kids come along to see Eric?' he asked. We nodded.

'Like a go on it?' he asked.

We didn't need asking twice. It was a magical ride. I had never seen anything quite like it. It wasn't as exciting as all the sorts of rides you see at modern fairs, but it was really special.

This time we lost Mo, Whizzer and Chip. Mo fell in love with the horses and Chip was fascinated by all the mechanics. Most surprising of all, Whizzer loved the music. It was nothing like rap, but he thought it was great. That left Sparky, Sam, Raj and myself to continue exploring. We looked in on all sorts of different things, coming across Angelica and Doug, but they were too busy talking to each other to bother with us.

At the far end of the Basin were some rowing boats. The owner said we could use them as long as we wore the life-jackets. Sparky and Raj took one boat, and Sam and I went in the other. We raced each other up and down the Basin until we were exhausted. Eventually Eric called us all back. He had been preparing a magnificent picnic, which we ate on the bank, together with a number of people from around the Basin.

I was amazed. These grown-ups seemed to know all about our crusade. They talked about the factory—and about the unfriendly attitudes of its staff. They all felt very angry about the factory, because there was still evidence of the pollution right down in the canal basin—nearly four miles away. Some of them had already written to the local newspaper, but nobody would listen to them—or perhaps someone or something was stopping them. Some of the grown-ups there said they would help us, if we needed help. All of a sudden, the man from the fairground ride burst into song. Eric played his mouth organ, and we all joined in the chorus. It was a great time, and it made me all the more determined to do something about the factory. Maybe we could write to the newspaper as well. Eric liked the new spot, but really wanted to get back to his old mooring and make that somewhere good for people to visit.

The journey home was good fun. We had our rock to eat, and we had some very happy memories. Doug dropped us off. He and Angelica were going somewhere the next day, and wanted to get back. They said they wouldn't be around for a couple of days in fact.

'Don't do anything silly while we're away,' said Doug meaningfully. 'Remember—be patient!'

I didn't answer!

I can be patient for at least five minutes, as long as I get what I want. The day after the visit to Eric's, Sam and I decided we had to *do* something. It was too bad that Doug and Angelica weren't there, and we couldn't wait for the more detailed results from the tests the professor and Miss Fox were doing.

We decided it was time to go to the local press. Most of the gang were busy, so just Sam and I made our way down into town to the local newspaper office. The building was down at the back of the bus station and was only a year old. It was all open-plan, and you could see a lot of the reporters at work from the reception desk.

'Can we see a reporter?' Sam asked.

'Sure, look, there's a whole load working over there,' responded a bored-looking receptionist.

'Oh, ha ha,' I said, adding, 'We think we have a very good story.'

'Sit there,' she said, pointing to a set of chairs.

She called over a man from the group of reporters

and spoke quietly to him. He came over to us.

'How can I help you, kiddies?' he said.

Yuk! *Kiddies!* Who did he think we were?

Sam blurted out our story and he listened. When Sam had finished he said, 'Thank you very much for the information. We'll put it on file.'

'Put it on file,' I repeated. 'Put it on file? You've got to do more than that. You've got to print it as a front-page story.'

'Look, young man', he replied. 'You are very short on evidence. That factory has brought a lot of work to the area, and the canal has been an eyesore for years.'

'So you're really going to do nothing?' Sam asked angrily.

The reporter just looked at us, then turned away.

'No wonder this paper is so useless,' I announced loudly to anyone who might be listening, and we both stormed out. I couldn't slam the door because it was automatic, but I did in my head!

We decided to try the City Hall. At least they should be interested. To begin with, it was almost impossible to find a councillor to talk to. There were so many people trying to stop you. There were security guards, receptionists, more security guards, and finally lots of doors to hide behind.

After what seemed like several hours of frustration, we eventually managed to find our way to a woman hiding behind several doors and a big desk. She said that she was the local councillor for the area where the factory was. She was totally disinterested in our story and said exactly the same thing as the reporter. It was all too much.

'If I was old enough to vote,' I announced grandly, 'there is no way that you would get my vote.'

This time the doors weren't too heavy, and I succeeded in banging quite a few before the security guards caught up with us. We got thrown out!

Sam and I sat silently on the City Hall steps. I began to wish I'd never fallen in the canal in the first place. 'So what do we do now?' demanded Sam.

I shrugged my shoulders. I was stuck!

The walk back to the club was long and silent. I kept trying to imagine what advice Doug would give. I couldn't think of anything except to have a meeting of the gang the next day. It sounded like a good plan, and it gave me time to think. Sam was so depressed that she didn't argue.

We had a Coke together and then set off home. I had a night's sleep to think of something. Would an idea come? I tried thinking. I tried writing things down, but the paper stayed blank. I even tried talking to myself, but that didn't get an answer either. I pulled loads of books down from the shelves and sprayed them over my bed.

Nothing!

Eventually I tried prayer. After that my brain was so tired that I fell asleep immediately.

17
Drama in the Streets

I woke up the next morning, still without an idea in my head, and with a pile of papers and books sprayed round the room. What a mess! My mum would go spare.

I set about tidying up when I suddenly saw, staring up from the local paper, THE ANSWER.

Because the City Festival had been so popular, it had been decided that the street theatre and acts would be allowed to continue throughout the summer. That's what we would do. A good bit of drama. Something eye-catching—with a message. I dashed around getting washed and dressed, made an effort at tidying up by throwing the books back on the shelves or in the cupboards, grabbed the paper, and hurtled out of the door.

I called Sam out of her house and outlined my plan. 'Look,' I said, pushing the paper into my hands.

'What?' she replied with a blank look on her face.

I pointed at the article in the paper. 'We are going to put on a play,' I said.

She looked at me as if I had a screw loose. I just

carried on. We would do a play on the City Hall steps as a protest. It was legal, and nobody could stop us. Maybe then people would take notice.

'What? *Us?*' she said, in disbelief. 'Since when did you get an Oscar?' Anyway, who is going to organize it and everything?'

I had thought of that.

'Get your bike,' I said, 'and meet me in ten minutes. We're going to see Eric and his mates. They offered to help, and they'd be good at that sort of thing.'

'Brilliant,' Sam said. 'But why ten minutes?'

'I've got to sort my room out,' I replied.

She blinked in shock! Then she offered to help. Between us we had it sorted in five minutes. I was going to get everything right this time.

We headed off on our bikes. After I showed my mum the room, she was happy to let me go! It was a long ride, but Sam was good company and the time passed quickly. When we arrived at the Basin we got the usual greeting from Walter, followed by a surprised look from Eric.

'What are you two doing here?' he asked.

I told him about my idea. I also told him about what happened with the councillors and the newspaper. He nodded a lot and listened. After a while he gave us a glass of home-made lemonade and left us. In about twenty minutes he was back with most of the people from the Basin.

We sat and watched while they started to get organized. 'Leave it with us.' The rock-makers ran us home in their van with the bikes in the back. Eric arranged to meet us at the club hut the next day. I couldn't wait to see what they were going to do.

The next day the gang all met at the hut. Sam and I told them about the plan and then we waited. It seemed ages before we heard anything, then, in the distance, we heard a bang, then another. Around the corner into Church Street came an old van, followed by another. The front van was decorated in all sorts of bright colours, and when they came to a stop, out came clowns, jugglers, and other assorted people in fancy dress.

Eric outlined the plan. They were going to do all sorts of acts—juggling, tumbling, tricks—around the City Hall, then when there was a big enough crowd they would perform a little play. All we had to do was to unroll some banners and walk round at the right moment.

It sounded fun if nothing else! We all got kitted out, then split up to make our way to the City Hall. It was quite safe because the area was large and traffic-free. The various clowns, jugglers and magicians began their work and soon had attracted a big crowd. They were so good that some of the people from inside City Hall came out to watch, including the Mayor.

On Eric's command a group formed on the steps and began to act a play. It started out like *Little Red Riding Hood*. But as it progressed, Red Riding Hood went to see her grandmother who was very worried about the canal that passed by her house. The wolf and his cubs who had been so charming turned nasty when Red Riding Hood asked them about all the mess in the canal. Then they turned around—and on their backs was written RAWSON MARSDEN LTD! It had the audience in stitches until Eric stopped it all.

He pulled out a megaphone and explained to the crowd what the play was all about. He was very good and the crowd started clapping him. Then he got us to unfurl the banners and the show was complete. CLEAN UP OUR CANAL, they said. STOP POLLUTION NOW.

The only people not smiling were the people from the Council. It wasn't long before they called in some of their own security guards and the police to move us on. But by that time we had got a huge crowd on our side. It was brilliant.

That wasn't the end of it either! Just at that moment along came Miss Fox and Professor Sprottles. They had been busy too. With them was the reporter who had been so horrible to us.

'What's happening?' asked Sam.

'We're going in to see the environmental health officer,' Miss Fox replied.

'We have enough evidence from the samples,' added Professor Sprottles, 'to force an inquiry, and we are going in with this reporter to see that it happens.'

The reporter just smiled weakly at me and Sam and looked away. I wasn't going to fuss—I was just happy that something was being done. I know we should have waited, but Sam and I couldn't resist skipping off from the fun at the City Hall and making our way to the factory. The rest of the gang followed. We arrived at the factory gate and I went straight up to Hargreaves.

'Clear off,' he ordered when he saw us, then added, 'What do you want anyway?'

'We want to see the manager,' I demanded.

'Clear off or I'll call the police,' he said.

We didn't try to get past him, but backed off, stood in the road, and unfurled our banners again. He went crazy, shouting at us. He didn't come after us because it was a public road and he would have been seen. Instead he went in his little hut to ring someone up.

No one came out, but it wasn't long before a police car came rolling up. Unfortunately, my dad was inside. He looked at me, looked at the banners, and groaned. I could feel the blood draining from my cheeks.

'Get in,' he ordered, opening the back door of the car.

'But Dad—' I started.

'Get in,' he said, louder this time.

He told the rest of the gang to go home, refusing to listen to Sam. Hargreaves looked satisfied. Dad didn't speak to me in the car, and he didn't take me home. Before long we turned into the yard of the police station.

'Sit there,' he said, motioning me to sit down on a bench, 'I'll deal with you later. At the moment there seems to be some bother around the City Hall.'

I didn't think it was wise just then to tell him that I had something to do with that as well. I sat there for hours while people came and went. Then through the door came Angelica and Doug.

Doug looked at me, but he was smiling. He went over to the desk and had a word with the man on duty. Doug and Angelica were taken through into an office, and Dad appeared. They seemed to be talking for ages, then two things happened. First of all, Dad came out.

'Well, you did it again,' he said. 'It looks as though Rawson Marsden needs investigating.' Then he said, 'Well done.' He gave me a hug and then went back to work. Doug and Angelica came out, and we made for the door.

Just at that moment the dreaded Hargreaves came in through the door, accompanied by two policemen. He just snarled at us as he was dragged in.

We left. Dad told me later that the Incredible Hulk had assaulted a police officer. And they were also investigating the burning of Eric's boat. Not to mention the inquiry which would be taking place . . .

I told Doug and Angelica what had been going on. They had arrived back to be told some of it by Sam and Eric, but had come to help me before getting all the details.

We all got back to the club hut to be met by the gang and Eric's friends. Everybody was a bit tired and we cleaned the fridge out of soft drinks. Eric was already making plans for his return, and for the setting up of his new business—boat repairs. He thought it wouldn't be long before narrow boats started using the canal again.

Some of his friends from the Basin were already talking about setting up a ferry service down to the canal basin for the people from the city. It all sounded great.

At the club hut the clowns and jugglers started to teach the gang how to perform. It was great fun. Nobody wanted to leave. Eric nipped out and got some more to drink, and it wasn't long before the singing started. There's nothing like an instant party.

I could see that there were only two people not really joining in. They were Angelica and Doug. They looked as if they were sitting on a secret and were about ready to burst. It didn't take long before we found out what it was.

Suddenly Doug stood on a chair and shouted for everyone to stop. It took ages because everybody was talking and singing and having a good time.

'I want to make an announcement,' he shouted, clearing his throat.

Everyone went quiet.

'Angelica and I are going to get married,' he said, with a big smile on his face.

There was total silence, then suddenly everyone cheered at once! Suddenly there was twice as much noise—cheering, singing, laughing and shouting. It went on for ages and only stopped when the door of the club opened. It was Dad again!

Everyone went quiet again.

'You've done something good today,' he said. 'But now you're making people in the street complain. Can you keep the noise down, please? There's such a thing as noise pollution, you know!'

That made everyone laugh.

When Dad found out that Doug had proposed to Angelica he smiled and shook their hands. Then he went down the street telling people, and before long quite a few people who lived in Church Street came in to congratulate them. Doug and Angelica had been off telling their parents—that's why they'd missed all the fun. They weren't missing any now. Everybody liked Doug, and everybody wanted to shake his hand.

We didn't get home till late, but nobody minded. It had been a great day!

18
A Perfect Party

Doug, Angelica and Eric decided to make one big 'official' party out of Eric's return up the canal and their engagement. It was going to be a great do.

The City Council had done an about turn, together with the factory owners. There was going to be an official enquiry, but already the factory was being cleaned up, the management changed, and all of the work that caused the pollution in the first place was being transferred to a new factory on the outskirts of the city. The company, together with the city council, was putting some money into a scheme that would transform the canal into a leisure area with walks and gardens. Eric was going to be given a special mooring, and he had been asked to start up a little museum about canal life. He was delighted.

As for Nick and Co.—well, it's not every day a gang appears on the front of the local newspaper with the headline: LOCAL CLUB SAVES CANAL. There was a photo. Even Wally looked like a noble hound in it.

But there was some bad news for the gang, too. Doug told us he was moving to another church when he and Angelica got married. They were going to Manchester, he told us. Angelica was moving her business as well. It was all very sad, but it wasn't happening straight away.

I wondered what would happen to the club, and I also wondered if it would change the way we did things. I had really grown very close to Doug. He had taught me a lot, even though I fought against him. I would miss him!

The day of the party came at last. We hadn't been allowed to help get it ready at all. We all assembled on Canal Street as instructed, but to our surprise, we were bundled into Doug's van and taken down the canal basin where Eric was waiting for us. His boat was decked out in balloons and garlands. Before we got on board we were all given clowns' hats and red noses. This was going to be good!

The trip up the canal was great, but as we came up to the wharf opposite the factory, we gasped at what we saw. There were tables of food and drink, and all around were the people from the Basin, dressed in circus gear, juggling, clowning, walking on stilts, all sorts of exciting things.

We had an absolutely magic time, with all the fun of the fair. Walter strutted around quacking in excitement and dressed in a brightly coloured bow. Mum and Dad arrived with Wally, and he was soon dressed in a bow to join in.

Then I saw the Professor and her husband. They

had dressed up in clowns' outfits too. They looked really funny, not at all like the clever people they were.

At last I saw the beautiful Miss Fox. *Jane!* She was dressed as a trapeze artist and was with a big bloke, who turned out to be her boyfriend, a rugby player. I decided to steer clear!

The food was delicious. Lump especially was enjoying every minute of it. But something had to go wrong. It was all too perfect. Something always went wrong at these events. Who was going to cause it this time? I looked around, but even Lump, the usual cause, seemed to be safely munching away.

Only Walter and Wally looked at all dangerous. They were in their usual mad moods and getting under everyone's feet.

'What's the matter with you?' Sam asked.

'It's all too perfect,' I replied. 'Something's got to happen.'

'Maybe not this time,' Sam said hopefully.

I put it out of my mind and joined in a spot of juggling. It looked so easy. But it needed such concentration. Once you started, it wasn't easy to stop. Suddenly things started to go wrong. It wasn't Lump, or Chip, or Whizzer that caused it—it was me!

Just for one second I took my eye off the balls I was juggling with to avoid stepping on Walter. That was the start of it all!

A ball shot out of my hand and caught another juggler on the shoulder. He was juggling with plates. One of them whizzed off in the general direction of Lump. It didn't hit him, but landed in a bowl of trifle in front of him. Lump, splattered with trifle, leapt back, knocking Whizzer over. Whizzer fell into a stilt walker, who tottered and swayed, before falling with great grace into the canal.

But that wasn't all. The stilts shot up in the air and knocked Chip's plate out of his hand. It sailed through the air and landed, complete with contents, neatly on my head! What could I say? This time the joke was on me. I started it and I well and truly got it in the end!

By the time it happened everybody was so happy they didn't really care. It was a fantastic party.

Later, when I'd managed to scrape off most of the flying food, Sam and I sat on the bank tossing pebbles into the canal. It felt like it was the end of something. I knew that things wouldn't be the same again. Especially after Doug left.

'I suppose we're growing up,' Sam said.

'I don't know whether I want to,' I replied.

It was a funny sort of feeling.

Sam put her head on my shoulder.

Then Sparky joined us, and before long the whole gang was there, sitting on the bank and throwing leftovers to the ducks. Eric told us it was the first time he'd seen ducks on this part of the canal for more than a year. Walter strutted up and down the bank, quacking in a superior way.

The rest of the summer we spent a lot of time helping Eric get things straight. He couldn't move into Angelica's workshop for another six months, so he concentrated on setting up a ferry service with his boat from Canal Street to the Basin. Most of the gang helped out and we all earned some useful extra pocket money.

The trial of Hargreaves was in the local press, and he was sent to prison for burning Eric's boat. The factory manager hadn't known what methods Hargreaves was using to get rid of Eric, so he didn't get a jail sentence, but he lost his job.

One of the good things that happened was an invitation to Professor Sprottles' house. Her husband taught me to play golf in the back garden until we had broken almost every pane in his greenhouse, but he didn't seem to care.

I decided it would be good to teach Doug. He tried very hard. We took some old golf balls onto a patch of waste ground and I tried to teach him everything that the doctor had taught me. He kept swishing very hard, but the ball didn't go very far.

Then, all at once, he got it right. Five times in a row he did a perfect shot as the ball flew to the safety of a big wire fence.

'This is great,' he said.

He spoke too soon. Taking your eye off the ball is a terrible mistake! Just as he was about to hit a particular beauty, along came Angelica.

That threw him.

Instead of flying to the safety of the fence, the ball shot off at an angle, hit a lump of concrete and flew gracefully in the direction of—yes, you've guessed it—some glass. Only this time it wasn't just *some* glass, it was a local double glazing merchant.

The sound wasn't so much a tinkle as an enormous KER-ASH!

Doug looked at me. He looked at Angelica.

'Leave it to me,' I said. 'Let me sort it out.'

What was I saying? But Doug looked so pathetic. However, before I reached the shop Doug had caught me up. 'We're in this together, Nick!' he said.

We looked at each other, took a deep breath, and opened the door!

THE NICK & CO. SERIES

Bob Croson

Trouble never seems to be far away when the irrepressible Nick Baker is around. No matter how good his intentions, Nick's brainwaves always seem to backfire, with unexpected and often hilarious results.

Whether their youth club is threatened with closure, they are on a camping holiday or their school is in trouble, Nick & Co. are always ready to spring into action. Nick has a Master Plan for every occasion, but somehow it never turns out quite as expected...

Nick & Co. in a Fix
ISBN 0 85648 953 0

Nick & Co. on Holiday
ISBN 0 7459 1346 6

Nick & Co. to the Rescue
ISBN 0 7459 1832 8

KATE AND THE MYSTERY PONIES

Sally Fielding

'Shasta. My lovely Shasta. She was really mine and I loved her.'

For Kate, it was like a wonderful dream. A horse of her own at last, and a chance to jump in the County Show. Then the suspicions crowded in. What was going on at the stables? She began to have doubts—was Shasta really hers after all? Was her dream about to become a nightmare?

A story for any girl who dreams of a pony of her own.

ISBN 0 85648 959 X

More stories from LION PUBLISHING for you to enjoy: